Spankee

Ronda DeMure

Published by Submission and Dominance, 2021.

Table of Contents

1. Chapter One: Coffee

UNABLE TO SUPPRESS a grin whenever she gazed at the "see you soon," message on her smartphone, Rebecca finally clicked it back to the home screen. 9:42am. The meeting was scheduled for ten o' clock but she had arrived at the coffee shop in plenty of time to find a strategic seat next to the picture window where she would be both out of the way yet able to watch as people approached the door. The morning at home had been routine, just like every other weekday morning. Nick left for work at seven following a quick peck and the cursory 'love you' and the girls, Susan and Deborah, boarded the school bus soon afterward, each clutching their paper bag containing a meticulously prepared lunch. Rebecca's life was the epitome of perfect; happy marriage, nice house, two well-adjusted kids. She had made her parents proud and was the envy of many of her friends. Why, then, had she spent the past two years secretly watching women being spanked on the internet? How did those innocent bouts of voyeurism evolve into her enrolling in a spanking site several months ago? She had initially never planned to become involved in chat but, fueled by a growing fantasy of being spanked herself, was soon spending upwards of an hour each morning corresponding anonymously with likeminded people. Chat soon led to filling out a profile, which led to email, which led to this morning. Her smartphone now showing 9:53, Rebecca wrested herself from musing and paid attention to the people approaching from the parking lot. There he was; six feet tall, salt and pepper hair in a pinstripe suit and carrying a black portfolio. He held the door open for a woman customer as she exited then strolled confidently inside and looked around. "Average looking, long dark hair, wearing a blue dress," was the description she had given to him yesterday and, when he looked her way, her smile provided the affirmation of who she was. "Rebecca?" He matched her smile. "I'm delighted to meet you."

Momentarily disarmed by his accent, Rebecca awkwardly slid to her feet before she was able to blurt out, "It's nice to finally meet you Don. You never told me you were English."

"I certainly hope that doesn't count against me." Don said jovially as he placed his portfolio on the table and extended his right hand towards the front counter. "How would you like your coffee?"

"Cream and two sugars, please."

"I'll be right back."

Rebecca watched Don intently as he ordered the coffees. His demeanor, the way he joked with the girl at the counter, even the way he stood at the counter exuded confidence. She smiled at him as he returned with two delicious looking pastries and two steaming mugs on the tray. "Relax, Rebecca," he said.

Was he also a mind reader?

"We're just two people here to chat and munch on these goodies." He picked up his black coffee. "No obligation, remember?" He took a quaff from the mug. "So, let's learn a little more about each other. Tell me, do you always go by Rebecca?"

"Pretty much. When I was a kid I went by Becky but I decided to be Rebecca about the time I got into high school."

"More grown up sounding?"

"Yes, that's exactly right." She recalled how she longed at that age to be older. She also admitted that now, after years of shouldering the responsibilities that went along with being an adult, she sometimes fondly remembered her carefree days as a girl. Don was a great conversationalist, he listened to her every word, and his friendly small talk lulled Rebecca into a comfortable sense of warmth, almost familiarity, with him. Her guard down, she soon freely opened up about her life, and then her frustrations; her sense of something missing, in spite of an outwardly ideal life. Within half an hour she was sufficiently relaxed to ask the question that had been tormenting her. "Can I ask you, Don," she quickly looked around then leaned across the table so she could whisper. "What it is you get out of spanking somebody?"

Don leaned back into his chair, cradling his coffee. "Pure pleasure," he said into her eyes. "I simply enjoy spanking for its own sake." He leaned forward again and added quietly, "Don't worry. I have no ulterior motive. You can be confident that if you choose to leave here with me it will be just for a spanking and nothing more."

Rebecca had very pointedly used the words "no sex" in her profile but in spite of that so many of the men who had contacted her insisted that sex was a necessary accompaniment to a spanking. Don had presented himself as a gentleman via email and he clearly was so in person. "Can we go now?" she asked coyly.

It was a short drive to Don's house and Rebecca stood nervously in the foyer as Don closed the front door behind them. He stood behind her, his hands cupping her shoulders, and whispered, "I want you to take off your dress," into her right ear. She immediately complied. For some reason, be it either Don's touch or his commanding accent, her nervousness had completely gone, and she happily handed over her dress then turned to face him in shoes and underwear. He told her to place her shoes by the door while he hung her dress in the hallway closet, and then instructed her to remove her bra. His matter-of-fact mannerisms were so calming that she it wasn't until he was hanging her bra next to her dress that she realized she had even taken it off. She stood attentively and pulled her shoulders back. For some strange reason she wanted him to notice her breasts.

But if Don did notice her breasts, it didn't show. He took her left wrist in his right hand, walked her slightly in front of him into the next room and positioned her in front of a large black leather couch. "Stand here," he said, "Hands behind your back." He then sat down in the middle of the couch, deliberately looking at her. "I like your panties," he exclaimed, nodding affirmatively at the white lace undergarment.

Her 'thank you' was immediate and genuine, yet at the same time that she spoke it she was trying to figure out why his saying that pleased her so much.

"I am going to pull them down, though," he told her, then leaned forward, reached out with both hands, and proceeded to do so.

In spite of her trembling and accelerated breathing, Rebecca tried to remain still and quiet and began to drift into a dreamlike state while her panties slid past her knees and dropped around her ankles. Other than Nick and her doctor, this was the only man who had ever seen Rebecca naked and the fact that she had met him less than an hour ago only served as an enhancement to her growing excitement.

Suddenly, she was face down across Don's lap. How did that happen? She felt his right hand massaging the pale flesh of her right buttock while his left hand gently caressed her shoulders and neck. By the time Don had moved his hand to the left side of her bottom, Rebecca was lulled and relaxed, her eyes mere slits. Don's words, "I believe you are now ready for your first spanking," seemed to be coming from far away.

The first slap was more audible than sensory, but was followed by a warm tingle right before the next one struck. The strokes were evenly placed and, after a dozen of them, Rebecca felt her whole bottom glowing. Unable to close her mouth, she could hear her breathing become more rapid as both the frequency and the intensity of the spanking increased. She involuntarily tried to push her shoulders upwards but Don's left hand on the back of her neck kept her at bay as he continued to spank her crimson behind. The fire now radiating from her bottom was spreading through the inside of her thighs, but it was not registering as pain. She couldn't describe it, it was a sensation she had never known before, and all she did know was that she didn't want it to stop. Not yet. Not until...she suddenly found herself straining in vain against Don's grip, writhing and trying and press her wanting pussy against his leg. In their email correspondence he had promised to permit her an orgasm when she was ready, and she most certainly felt that she was. Clearly, however, the determination of 'readiness' was not to be hers.

"Not yet. I'm going to give you six more strokes first," Don told her, completely unaffected by her gasping and struggles. "And they're going to be good ones."

Those last strokes came down hard and, her mouth wide open in response to them, Rebecca pushed with all she could muster against his left hand, but with her hands unable to make solid contact with the floor her effort was futile. Immediately after the last stroke, though, Don informed her that he now intended to follow through on his promise. Rebecca tried to spread her legs in anticipation as she felt Don's hand move between them. His thumb effortlessly slid inside her, instantly finding her engorged g-spot while two fingers alighted on her clitoris. His simple squeeze was all that was necessary. Rebecca exploded noisily into the most intense orgasm she had even known, her whole body tightening in ecstasy accompanied by a previously unknown primal scream before she collapsed limpid back across Don's lap. Don slowly removed his hand and soothed her glowing bottom with her abundant moisture before effortlessly flipping her face-up. He cuddled her into his lap, her knees up as he leaned back onto the couch, enveloping her in his left arm. She could feel his breath and the gentle touch of his right hand toying with her hair while she nuzzled contentedly into the nape of his neck. "Well, Rebecca," Don whispered after several quiet minutes. "You've now been spanked."

When Deborah and Susan came home from school later that afternoon they found their mother in a wonderful mood, insisting on taking them out for ice cream instead of the normal routine of setting them about their homework, simply saying they could do it later that evening. The girls, of course, did not object. When Nick slid between the sheets that night to assume the missionary position on top of his wife he was thrilled with Rebecca's affectionate responsiveness, completely unaware of the effect that his vanilla routine was having on her still warm bottom as he pounded it against the bottom sheet. Satisfied, he rolled off her and, after an obligatory kiss, instantly fell asleep. Rebecca, however, lingered as long as she was able in that disconnected pre-sleep zone trying to comprehend her muddled thoughts. The spanking had been everything she'd hoped for, but it had brought with it an unexpected bonus, a consequence actually. She had never expected that being spanked could enhance her regular life. Rebecca's earlier assuredness that a one-time spanking would satisfy her so she could then put it behind her was being called into question as she subjected that previous thinking to the fluid analysis of slumber.

2. Chapter Two: Conflict

DON RESPONDED TO THE text message with the question, "I thought you just wanted a one-time experience?" It had been a week since he had spanked Rebecca and, while he was pleased to hear from her again, he was also surprised. She had been very clear in all their correspondence prior to meeting that she simply wanted to know firsthand what it was like to be spanked. She was a happily married woman with a secret fantasy to fulfill and, once done, that was to be it.

Rebecca's return text was almost immediate: "I'm a bit confused about things. Can we meet for coffee and talk?"

"It would be my pleasure; how about 10am tomorrow, same place?"

"I'll be there. Thanks."

It was a few minutes to ten when Rebecca, dressed in a gray sheer-front blouse, blue jeans and silver faux snakeskin heels, arrived at the coffee shop. Don was already sitting at the same table where they first met. He immediately rose on seeing her walk in and gave her a welcoming hug. "I have your coffee all ready," he said, nodding towards the tabletop as she sat down. "It's rather quiet in here today." He sat opposite her and continued in a slightly quieter voice, "So no-one can listen in on our conversation."

"That's good." Rebecca sipped at her coffee. "Mmm, just the way I like it."

"I aim to please."

"Oh, you do that very well." She responded without thought, then buried her face into her coffee mug in an attempt to hide an instant blush.

Don just smiled, brushed the lock of raven hair that had flopped across her face back behind her left ear and waited for her to look up again. "You liked being spanked, then?" he teased.

"I liked it way too much, actually."

"I see." Don leaned back into his chair and picked up his coffee, his eyes not leaving her face.

"And therein lays my conflict." She cradled her drink in both of her hands. "For a couple of days afterward it made things so much better at home." She quickly looked over her shoulder to make sure nobody had sat at a close by table before continuing. "Sex, I mean. I actually came with my husband."

"Hmm, that's good; yet I sense there must be a 'but' coming."

"But it didn't last, so now I'm back to my toys while I watch spanking online." She twisted her mouth. "Except that toys and voyeurism isn't doing it for me anymore."

"Now that you know how much you like it, why not ask your husband to spank you?"

"I did, but he said that was sick and that I must be watching too much daytime television. He told me that if you love someone you don't go around beating on them. Trust me; this is not a concept that Nick is ever going to get." She vibrated her head. "It's not even worth trying." Rebecca deliberately placed her mug in front of her and put both of her hands on the tabletop. "So, I came up with an idea." She looked directly at Don. "Would you consider spanking me on a somewhat routine basis?"

"You're suggesting that we have an ongoing relationship?"

"Yes," her head tilted to the left and she tried to suppress a smile, "Just for spanking."

"So instead of your one-time fantasy, you feel you'd now like to become a regular spankee, eh?"

"Yes, I would; but still without sex."

Don looked thoughtful and took a swig of coffee. "I take it that by 'without sex' you're just referring to vaginal intercourse?" He put his mug down. "I am rather partial to a former president's definition of what constitutes sex, you know."

"I'd wondered about that." Rebecca made a security clutch on her coffee mug and stared at her hands. "That's the biggest part of my problem; I don't want to cheat on Nick."

"What's Nick's take on Clinton?"

Rebecca burst into laughter. "What Nick thinks," she raised her right index finger until she brought her chuckling under control. "He refers to him 'president pervert.'" Still grinning, she shook her head. "All we do is straight, missionary. Nick says oral is disgusting."

"What about you? What are Rebecca's thoughts?"

"Well," she blushed again. "There was this one time in college after I'd been drinking." Rebecca looked up, a coy smile extending to her eyes. "Maybe, down the road," she said. "But I don't want to at this point." She slid her right hand across the table until it touched Don's left and murmured. "Would that be okay?"

Don's eyes motioned to the crowd that had just entered the coffee shop and were filling up the tables. "Let's continue this conversation at my house," he said. "I have excellent coffee there, too."

"You'll have to excuse the mess in the kitchen," Don explained as Rebecca stared at the fresh drywall. "I'm in the middle of having it re-done. The floor is all finished, and they'll be back tomorrow to finish the walls." He spread his arms out. "By Wednesday this is going to look perfect." He beckoned to the table and chairs in front of the window overlooking the garden. "Have a seat," he said and proceeded to grind some coffee beans.

"I do like the floor," Rebecca said, admiring the red clay tiles. "What are the walls going to look like?"

"I want to have a natural, almost outdoorsy feel in here, so it will be wallpaper with a light-colored brick and ivy design."

The espresso machine forced the rich liquid into the carafe with a satisfying whoosh and Rebecca tasted the aroma while Don frothed the milk. He prepared the cappuccinos as if he were creating a work of art, adorning them with freshly grated nutmeg and chocolate before presenting them in front of her on the table. "Voila!"

"I've never had cappuccino," Rebecca admitted as she raised the cup to her lips. "Mmm, delicious," she looked up with a froth covered lip. "You're spoiling me."

"And I'd like to continue to do so. Perhaps you'd also enjoy being introduced to some implements which can be used in conjunction with spanking. I have a leather crop that I'm rather partial to, for example. It makes a most wonderful sound."

Rebecca's legs separated under the table as she squirmed in her seat. Why did his words have that effect on her?

"I suspect you might like that." He added, teasingly.

Rebecca finished her drink and licked her top lip to remove the last bit of froth. "May I use your restroom?" she asked.

"Certainly," Don replied, still sipping at his cappuccino. "Just down the hallway on the right."

Rebecca scurried away with a wry smile, returning only a few minutes later without her blue jeans on and her panties dangling from the fingertips of her right hand. She was still wearing the gray blouse but in place of the pink floral bra, which had been so delightfully evident beneath the flimsy material previously, her nipples were now begging for escape against the fabric. The blouse was long enough to cover the top part of her thighs but the darkness of her neatly trimmed pubic mound was clearly visible through it. Eyes averted, Rebecca extended her right hand towards Don, offering her panties to him as she softly murmured, "Please."

To her delight, Don took her hands in his, coaxing her to look up into his eyes. He took the panties from her and placed them on the table. "I want you to stand in the middle of the room," he began. "Now, bend over and hold the calves of your legs. That's right."

The blouse tickled as it slid across Rebecca's bottom, completely exposing it by the time she was bent over. Her leg muscles were tight, but her thought was not of any discomfort, she simply hoped that Don was enjoying this view of her legs. Always the person in charge of things around her house, here she liked being told what to do and realizing that she was posing for Don's pleasure was strangely exhilarating. Why was it so important to please him?

"Look at the straps of your shoes," Don continued. "See how they're buckled around your ankles? I want you imagine your wrists are also attached to them. Now, look towards me."

Rebecca's face turned up and the audible click of Don's camera committed her priceless expression and perfect pose to posterity. "Don't worry," he assured her as he stood and walked towards her. "That's just for me."

Rebecca looked down again in anticipation as Don moved silently behind her. She felt something soft brushing upwards against the back of her thighs and tightened her grip. If only her wrists really were attached, she mused. How much better that would be that she would no longer have to consciously keep hold and simply enjoy Don touching her.

"This is a crop," Don explained as he moved it upwards to lightly stroke her buttocks. "As you can see, it consists of a delightful piece of leather which is capable of providing you with a most pleasant sensation."

"Mmm." Rebecca's eyes were slits.

"And yet."

Rebecca felt a light tapping on her bottom followed by the sound of a quick snap.

"It can also be quite useful in getting your attention."

Suddenly, the area that had been tapped was afire, but her senses had been drawn to another area already being tapped. The next snap preceded another bite on the opposite cheek and after six strokes had fallen in rapid succession her entire bottom was hot.

"Hold this for me," Don said as he pushed the shaft of the crop sideways into Rebecca's mouth. She was thankful for something to bite down on.

"Very nice," he examined and caressed her hot bottom. "We have a most even patina.' He gave each cheek a swat with his right hand then reached down, removed the crop from her mouth and took her left hand in his right. "You can stand up now," he said, and pulled her towards himself as she did. Don's left arm around her shoulders, Rebecca snuggled the side of her face into his chest while his right hand massaged her bottom. "Now that you're nicely warmed up," he whispered. "I'd better take you to the couch."

Rebecca eagerly snuggled face down across Don's lap, soothed by his continued caressing of her still warm bottom. The first slaps seemed to flow out of the caresses but then increased in intensity with each subsequent stroke. Why was the heat from her bottom not registering as pain? How could she be so relaxed and yet so sexually aroused at the same time? Unable to fully comprehend the myriad of sensations she instead simply yielded to them and drifted into an almost dreamlike, disconnected state while Don continued his ministrations. It was her own increased breathing and feeble attempt to squirm against Don's left hand that returned her to awareness; the awareness that her whole body was trembling with desire. That the fire from her bottom was also consuming her clitoris and it was in desperate need of relief. "Please." It was barely a whisper falling out of her open mouth. "Please make me cum." Rebecca had never uttered those words before. Never been in a situation where someone else had that degree of control over her. She would have been willing to beg if Don had told her to, but he made no demands of her. Instead she was rewarded with his hand between her legs and she gushed against him as who knows how many fingers effortlessly slid between her engorged pussy lips. She was completely spent before he removed them, and he permitted her to remain in the delight of afterglow across his lap while he used her moisture to soothe her crimson bottom until she was once again able to speak.

"Do you remember, at our first meeting, you asked me what I got out of this?" Don asked.

"Yes?" Rebecca wrapped her arms around Don as she curled up in his lap.

"I like one-time encounters; spanking a woman I've just met is exciting for me. I've had no interest in developing a relationship in the past because I don't want to take away from that excitement, that newness." He kissed the top of her head. "But I do like you, Rebecca. You respond so well to being spanked. So," he leaned back into the couch and stroked her hair with his right hand, "If we were to make it different each time, we may just be able to figure out a way to make an ongoing spanking relationship work."

Rebecca looked up. "How would we make it different?"

"When you look at spankings online, do you ever come across role playing scenes?"

Rebecca suddenly became aware of her heart beating. How did he know? Was she that transparent to him? "I love watching role plays," she gasped.

"Tell me your favorite."

There was something about the way he asked that caused Rebecca's face to turn crimson and she bit at her lower lip, unable to respond, and tried to bury her head into his chest. Don gently hooked her chin with his right index finger, coaxing her face up to look at his again. "Schoolgirl?" he asked softly, to which she vigorously nodded.

"I'm so pleased," Don's smile was contagious. "Do you have a uniform?"

"My eldest daughter and I are about the same size. And she goes to catholic school so, yes. I could use one of her old uniforms."

"Splendid! I'd like you to come back here one day next week and bring it with you; you can change after you arrive. Be a 'schoolgirl' and you will meet the 'headmaster.'" Don nodded slowly and smirked. "He knows precisely how to deal with naughty schoolgirls."

"Wednesdays are always the best days for me."

"Then Wednesday it is." Don smiled broadly at Rebecca; her unasked question was so evident. "You don't have to worry about any impropriety; the headmaster is simply going to discipline you."

3. Chapter Three: Spanking

WEDNESDAY COULDN'T come soon enough for Rebecca. As soon as the girls had left for school, she folded up one of Deborah's old uniforms into a canvas bag and tucked behind the driver's seat of her car. It was now time for a shower. Don's instructions had been very specific; she was to be completely free of makeup and perfume, and complying was providing her with an odd, almost liberating, sensation. She smiled at herself in the mirror as she dried her hair, then quickly dressed in a blouse and blue jeans and was soon on her way to Don's house.

When the front door opened, she eagerly scurried inside clutching the bag with both hands. Don smiled at her and gestured to the bathroom at the end of the hallway. "Take your time," he said, "Then come and knock on my office door when you're ready."

In order to get ready in the bathroom Rebecca was to completely strip, which included removing all of her jewelry. She hung her clothes in the small cupboard, carefully placed her watch, earrings and wedding ring into a small pouch she had brought with her and tucked it inside her purse, and then put the purse in the cupboard and closed the door. She then opened the canvas bag and first took out the white panties that Don had liked so much on their previous session and slid them on. Don told her that she did not need to wear a bra and she enjoyed the sensation of the white cotton blouse on her already aroused nipples as she buttoned it up. Once dressed, she fluffed her hair back behind her ears and proceeded down the hallway to Don's office, her combination excited/nervous feeling now impacting her breathing. Don told her she would feel this way before the scene began, explaining it to her as quite natural trepidation. But he had also assured her that, once she was inside his office that feeling would give way to her, as he called it, "being in the moment." Rebecca stood nervously outside the door, very much hoping that was going to be the case. She took a deep breath and knocked.

"Enter." The reply was immediate and matter-of-fact. Rebecca's trembling hand turned the knob, and as soon as she was inside, she closed the door behind her. Don, now the headmaster for this role play, was sitting behind an oversized oak desk. He raised his right hand and beckoned her with two fingers, then silently watched without expression as she walked across the rug to stand attentively in front of the desk, her hands clasped behind her back and her eyes looking down at her shiny black shoes. Rebecca suddenly became very aware of the twelve inches of naked leg between the top of her socks and the hem of her pleated skirt, yet that feeling of vulnerability was also incredibly exhilarating.

"It has come to my attention, young lady," the headmaster's deep English accent boomed, "That you not only neglected to refer to the mathematics instructor as 'sir' but, when he verbally reprimanded you for it, you proceeded to suggest he 'get over it.'" He paused. "Is this correct?"

"I'm sorry, Sir." The mumbled words were out before Rebecca realized she had even spoken them. Why was she so naturally falling into this role of a schoolgirl, apologizing to something she had not actually done?

"I should very much hope so, young lady. It is now my responsibility to instill in you that such insubordination will not be tolerated." The headmaster leaned back into his leather chair.

Rebecca bit at her lower lip as her hands clenched tighter together.

"Since this is the first time I've had occasion to see you in my office, I suspect we do not need to resort to a caning this time. I shall provide you instead with a spanking which I trust will serve as a reminder to mind your manners in the future. Do you understand?"

"Yes, Sir. Thank you, sir."

"Very good." The headmaster stood up. "You will now bend over the desk."

Those words causing her breathing to accelerate, schoolgirl Rebecca stepped forward and leaned across the desktop, her arms above her head, while the headmaster walked around and stood to her left side. She closed her eyes and squirmed involuntarily as she felt her skirt being lifted and laid across her back. This was so much better than watching on the internet. The headmaster had not even touched her, yet she was already tingling between her legs and her aroused nipples were further stimulated by every movement as she pushed them against the desk.

"These are not regulation panties, girl." A swat to her right buttock accompanied the headmaster's stern words.

Rebecca had worn them because Don had previously liked them but, at this moment, he was not Don and she was not Rebecca. That realization instantly disconnected her from her former self and at that moment she was the schoolgirl, compliantly apologetic as the headmaster slid her offending panties to her ankles and proceeded to discipline her wanting bottom. The first two strokes hurt but she suppressed the urge to cry out, instead concentrating on the rush of warmth radiating over her backside. When the flow of warmth met the tingle, she no longer registered the slaps as pain but as something else. Something she had no words for. Did it hurt? Under other circumstances it might have but here, here it was pure excitement. Her panting increased until she could no longer close her mouth and her fingers clawed at the wooden desk as her body shuddered. The headmaster stopped spanking and massaged her flaming bottom until she became limp, then sat down in one of the wooden chairs in front of his desk. "Stand up, girl," he instructed.

She pushed herself to her feet and turned to face him, her panties still around her ankles.

"We still have another offense to deal with, don't we, young lady?"

"You mean, um, my lace panties, Sir?"

"Indeed! They belie an exhibitionist streak in you, since that could be the only possible reason for wearing them." He brought his fingertips together. "So, before I provide you with your reminder to dress appropriately in the future, I shall give you an opportunity to also contemplate this unsavory tendency. Do you see the hook on the back of the door?"

"Yes. Yes, I do, Sir."

"Hang your panties on it."

Rebecca stepped out of them, her mind scrambling as to what the headmaster might be referring to as time to contemplate. It sounded like he was going to eventually spank her again, but what was to come first?

"Now your blouse."

"Sir?"

"Hang your blouse on the hook."

Rebecca had been excited when Don had stripped her before, but as a schoolgirl being ordered to take her clothes off in front of the headmaster she was strangely embarrassed. She removed her blouse but instinctively covered her breasts with her hands as she turned to face him. He made no comment about her apparent shyness and simply told her to also hang her skirt on the hook, then watched as she turned her back to him and fumbled with the waistband.

"You will now stand right here," the headmaster pointed to spot in the middle of the carpet a yard in front of where he was sitting. "Place your feet eighteen inches apart and your hands behind your head. You will remain in that position for five minutes."

The excitement of being a humiliated schoolgirl was more than Rebecca could conceal and she panted as beads of liquid trickled down the inside of her naked thighs while she stood as still as possible, the headmaster simply looking at her without expression and saying nothing. After a long five minutes, he rose and walked behind her, stroked his hand across her crimson buttocks, then stood to her right side. "I am now going to provide you with punishment for incorrectly wearing your uniform," he said. "And since your bottom has already been spanked, I will administer it to your front."

Rebecca sucked in a deep breath through her partially open mouth, the realization of what was about to happen gushing into her already over stimulated mind.

"Six slaps should be sufficient." The headmaster watched her trembling face then added rhetorically, "Don't you agree?"

As his hand made repeated contact with the moisture between Rebecca's legs, she was unable to contain her gasps but managed to remain standing. The fourth slap brought her to what she thought was the edge or orgasm but the remaining two only inched her that much closer. She wanted another slap, just one more might do it, but the headmaster had completed his discipline. Eyes almost closed, her trembling body began to rock back and forth until the headmaster took hold of her right arm to steady her. "I can't possibly allow you to remain in this state, can I?" he asked softly.

"Please, sir..." she panted.

"You'd better drop your hands and lie down on the rug," he said, easing her to the floor. She lay down on her back, arms at her sides and her feet slightly apart facing the chair the headmaster had previously been sitting on. She looked up quizzically. The chair he was now sitting on. What was he doing? She desperately needed to be touched.

"Since it would be inappropriate for me to touch you," the headmaster said matter-of-factly, cradling his fingertips, "I give you permission provide yourself with relief. You may proceed."

Rebecca bit her lower lip. Masturbation had always her secret and it was private, no-one had ever seen her touch herself and even if Nick had wanted to watch she would have absolutely refused him. Yet, here, her right hand already having found its way to her quivering mound, there was no thought of embarrassment. With the expert manual dexterity Rebecca had developed over years of married life she earnestly brought herself to merciful orgasm while headmaster, sitting quietly only a few feet away, was afforded an unobstructed view of her fingers dancing with abandon between her now spread legs.

4. Chapter Four: Becky

DON INSTRUCTED REBECCA to take a day to reflect on their role play and told her they would meet at the coffee shop on Friday to discuss how she felt about it, as well talk more about the spanking relationship she had proposed earlier. Nothing else occupied her mind during that time interval. The sex with Nick the night following the spanking had, once again, been exceptional; her clitoris and g-spot, in an elevated state of arousal due to the discipline received from the headmaster, delivered her into multiple orgasms before her husband had finished with her. Furthermore, she had no qualms that it had been another man who had made it so: it was a naughty schoolgirl that had been spanked, not Rebecca. She liked that disconnect very much and was delighted that it became the first topic of discussion when she met with Don.

"I want to know your feelings about the different times I've spanked you." Don began. "What was different between them for you?"

"The first time was exciting, but I also felt a twinge of guilt afterwards. That's why it took me a week of agonizing over it before I contacted you again. But I felt no guilt at all after last time and you even had me masturbate in front of you. "Rebecca's face beamed. "Is that what happens, the more you do something the less you feel guilty about it?"

"Do you know why I had you remove your makeup and jewelry?"

"So I'd be a more authentic schoolgirl?"

"Partially true, but also to remove your identity as Rebecca and enable you to more effectively assume that role."

"And it worked. It was almost like I was watching someone else."

"That's why there was no guilt. If it had been Rebecca getting spanked you most likely would have been torn over that same guilt again, but as 'someone else' it is not Rebecca that is being spanked." Don paused and looked across the table; he had Rebecca's rapt attention. "Did you like being a schoolgirl?"

"Very much," Rebecca wished she hadn't responded so readily and, slightly embarrassed, her fingers began to absentmindedly fondle her face. "I liked everything about it," she added quietly, speaking to her coffee cup. "You know, I would have done anything you, the headmaster, told me." She looked back up at Don. "Why was that?"

"Because, in addition to wanting to be spanked, I believe you're also a submissive."

"How can that be?" Rebecca was taken aback. "Aren't submissive women supposed to be mindless airheads? I'm a college graduate; I manage all of our finances at home. I'm even the president of our PTA."

Don raised his right hand. "That's a common misconception. The fact is that many submissives are in demanding and even high profile, take charge positions. Being submissive provides them with a temporary escape from all of that," he smiled and slowly nodded, "As well a giving them the vehicle to get spanked."

"Wow! I never knew that." Rebecca shifted in her seat. "So?" She began sheepishly. "What else happens to submissive women? Besides getting spanked, I mean."

"Just about anything they want. The submissive defines her limits, tells her dominant what she wants to experience and turns herself over to him. It's a balance of vulnerability and trust."

Don's use of the word "vulnerability" instantly induced wetness between Rebecca's legs and she tightly crossed them. "I think I could trust you," She said, then rolled her teeth across her lower lip. "I get to define the limits?"

"That's correct." Don took a long drink of coffee and his eyes seemed to sparkle as his face re-emerged from the cup. "But limits do tend to be fluid. They change over time and, as trust grows, certain limits might be challenged." He put his cup down. "Except for hard limits; they're inviolate."

"So if I said sex is a hard limit?" Rebecca whispered excitedly.

"Then it would remain so. Only you could change that. A true dominant will never challenge a submissive's hard limit."

Rebecca untangled her legs, put her elbows on the table and rested her chin on top of her hands, a fruitless attempt to control her smirking. "Will I always get to be a schoolgirl?" she asked.

"Possibly." Don stroked his chin. "It's a role you clearly like, but it's a bit limited. We need to allow for variations." His grin grew as the idea came to him. "You are interested in disconnecting from Rebecca, right?"

"Absolutely! If there is no Rebecca, there's no guilt."

"You told me that when you were young you used to go by Becky, that Rebecca is your grownup name."

"That's right." She knew where this conversation was going and she very much liked it, involuntarily tapping her thighs together as she listened intently to Don's seductive accent.

"Then become Becky. Sometimes she can be a schoolgirl but other times she'll be doing things with her favorite uncle, Uncle Don."

"Will, um, Uncle Don touch Becky. You know, like you do?" It was an embarrassing question, but she needed to ask. "I didn't mind playing with myself in front of the headmaster," he added quietly, "But I liked it much better when you made me cum."

"Uncle Don will keep that in mind. It sounds like that might be an excellent reward for when somebody has been a good girl."

"Mmm," Rebecca squirmed in her seat. "What does it mean to be a good girl?" She desperately wanted to be one.

"Good girls are attentive and responsive." Don seemed to be smiling from his eyes. "And, of course, they are always obedient."

"Do they get to go for rides in your car?" She asked while looking through the window at Don's red convertible parked just outside.

"They might if they ask nicely."

"Uncle Don," Rebecca said dreamily, squirming into the back of her chair. "Will you take me for a ride in your car?"

"It would be my pleasure."

Rebecca slid onto the tan leather set while Don held the passenger door open for her. "Where are we going, Uncle Don?" she cooed.

"First," he looked at her and playfully shook his head. "I'm taking you shopping for some appropriate clothing." He started the car. "No niece of mine dresses in blue jeans when she is with me."

They strolled through the aisles of the department store together, Rebecca carrying the items that Don selected and handed to her: a light blue dress from the junior department, pretty lace knee socks and cute pink pumps. They last stop was the lingerie department. After Don asked, a bit louder than Rebecca would have liked, about her size she stood next to him with rosy cheeks while he selected a set of pastel colored cotton bikinis. "That should do it," he announced as he placed the panties on top of the bundle she was carrying, and then guided her to the checkout.

"Shopping for your daughter?" the clerk innocently commented as she made the tally. Don, quite unaffected and calm, made small talk and paid while Rebecca felt a fiery blush explode across her entire face. Still, once they were back in car her embarrassment quickly gave way to excitement. They were going to Don's house so she could model the purchase for him.

"Now, there's my girl." Don's voice was filled with approval as Rebecca entered the living room where he was relaxed on the large black leather couch. She stood in front of him with her hands behind her back, gently swaying from side to side, thoroughly enjoying his ogling her. Nick never looked at her anymore and it felt so good to be looked at. The bodice of the dress hugged her just enough to outline her breasts and allow a slight protrusion of nipple through the thin fabric, then flared out from a high waist to end six inches above her knees. Each sway flipped it up a couple of inches more.

"Show me your panties."

She grinned, eagerly moving her hands to the hem while constantly watching Don's delight, and teasingly raised the front of the dress until she was holding it completely up.

"I see you selected the blue."

"I'm saving the white for my schoolgirl uniform," she giggled, but remained still.

"The trouble is," Don leaned forward and stroked the back of his right index finger against the cotton stretched against the moist mound between her legs, "They appear to be wet." He looked up at her face. "I'm afraid I'm going to have to remove them and spank you, you naughty girl."

Rebecca was trembling and panting as she desperately tried to remain still while Don pulled her panties down her legs. Thankfully, she was soon face down across his lap, making no attempt to conceal that she was on the verge of orgasm after only a few minutes of spanking. Don continued spanking her, however. Hard. All he had to do was to touch her just right, the way he had done before, but he kept on spanking her. Gasping, she tried to wriggle but his left hand on the back of her neck kept her pinned while he continued his ministrations to her almost unbearably hot buttocks. She had never been so close yet unable to do a thing about it. Don had complete control. She closed her eyes to this realization and suddenly all that existed was the sound of his hand against her blazing flesh, incrementally riding her along an asymptote with each stroke: his to spank into infinity if he so desired. She understood. Her body relinquished the struggle and Don effortlessly slid two fingers into her, continuing to hold her down with his left hand as she screamed and bucked in uninhibited, ecstatic gyrations.

"Does this mean you're agreeing to a spanking relationship with me, then?" Rebecca's eyes were hopeful. Now dressed again, her still hot bottom encased in her blue jeans, and sitting with a cold drink in his kitchen, all she could think about was being able to come back and do this again.

"Perhaps." Don smiled. "I'd very much like to, but there are two provisions that will have to be met. "He teased her with the pause. "But, of course, they are completely up to you. Number one, I want you completely shaved."

"So I'll look like a girl?" Rebecca had no problem with this at all. Most of the women she watched getting spanked on the internet were smooth but, until now, there had been no reason for going through the trouble. Nick wouldn't care. He probably wouldn't even notice.

"Because that is the look I want for Becky."

"Okay. I'll do that." Doing what Don wanted was not only incredibly arousing but it also pleased her; she still didn't understand why, but it was a feeling she was beginning to reconcile with.

"Number two; you'll be Becky both in name and action." He raised his hand to cut off any words she was about to utter. "Don't say anything now. I want you to go home and think about it, and then send me your answer via email."

The question Rebecca had wanted to ask him was one of clarification. She suspected she knew what Don meant, but confirming the alternative meaning of Becky on the internet didn't take away from her combination of shock and concern. She had no experience in this regard. Still, it would be Becky doing it, not her. Rebecca could never bring herself to such humiliation. It wasn't something she even wanted for Becky, but she was compelled to admit that there was a certain degree of fairness to Don's position. It was a clear case of quid-pro-quo. She thought about it during the night and the next morning sent Don a text to confirm that she understood what it was that he wanted and to determine how far Becky would have to go. "Will uncle want to cum in Becky's mouth?" It might not be so bad if Becky didn't have to perform to completion.

Don's response was almost instant. "Yes."

"Is he going to make her swallow?" Maybe she wouldn't have to. She held the device in both hands awaiting the reply.

"That's what good girls do with their favorite uncles."

That afternoon Don received an email from a new sender. It was written in pink italics and a large, flowery font: "Hi Uncle Don. I'm so looking forward to being a good girl for you next Wednesday. Your niece, Becky."

5. Chapter Five: Good Girl

UPON ARRIVING AT DON'S house Rebecca was instructed to go upstairs to the guest bedroom, told she could take whatever time was necessary to become Becky and to come down when she was ready. She eagerly stuffed all her jewelry in her purse, completely stripped and hung her Rebecca clothing and purse in the closet. It was such a relief to shut the closet door; both identity and responsibility disappeared with the click of the latch and she was now free to be Becky.

The outfit that Don had laid out for her on the bed was a schoolgirl uniform, but very different to Deborah's old one that she had worn previously. This white blouse was made of thinner cotton and had no tails so it could not be tucked in and it was just long enough to reach to the waistband of the pleated, red plaid skirt. The skirt itself was considerably shorter, sixteen inches from waist to hem. White cotton bikini panties, green plaid knee socks and black buckle-up shoes completed the ensemble. Dressed, she admired herself in front of the full-length mirror. There was no thought of Rebecca at all and it was pure Becky who subsequently descended the stairs, smiling at Uncle Don standing at the bottom and wondering if he was able to see up her skirt. Hoping he was looking. Wanting him to look.

"There you are, Becky." Uncle wrapped his left arm around her shoulders and lightly pulled her to his chest in an affectionate hug. Head happily against this shoulder, she flitted her eyes up to look up at him. She was a girl again and it was indescribably wonderful.

"How would you like a milkshake?" Uncle Don asked.

"Strawberry?" she replied, excitedly.

"Strawberry it is!"

Becky followed her uncle into the kitchen and slid up onto one of the two stools at the tall table in front of the window, her right leg dangling teasingly as she watched him assemble the ingredients at the center island.

"Can I ask you a question, Uncle?" Beck asked coyly, her right leg swinging back and forth.

"Of course you may, Becky. I want you to feel free to ask me anything."

"How come boys like to look up girl's skirts?"

'It's just natural."

"Do you like to?"

"I do when she is as pretty as you." Uncle Don dolloped whipped cream onto each of the milkshakes, topped each with a maraschino cherry, inserted straws and served them with a flourish. Becky dove in at hers, sucking at the straw until she had drawn up a third of the milkshake, then eased back, picked up the cherry and popped it in her mouth. "Delicious milkshake, uncle," she said. "Thank you."

"You are most welcome, Becky." He chucked, in no way concealing that he was looking to the side of the table. "Tell me, do you like teasing boys by swinging your leg like that?"

"Kind of, yeah," she slurped her milkshake and added, "But I don't let them see my panties."

"No?"

"Liz got caught showing Brian her panties and she was sent to the headmaster." Becky took a noisy draught of her drink. "It got her a good spanking."

"And rightfully so, that's completely inappropriate behavior at school." Uncle Don looked thoughtful as he drank, and then he began to reminisce, "When I was a boy at school in England, we used to offer a girl half a crown to get her to lift up her skirt for us. That's sort of like an American quarter."

"Steve gave me a dollar," Becky blurted out proudly, then slapped her hand across her mouth as Uncle Don gave her a look which made it unnecessary for him to utter a word.

"Umm, it was in the stairwell," she explained, "No-one else saw." She looked worried. "You won't tell mom, will you?"

"What would she do?"

"Probably ground me for life." She noisily slurped the last of her milkshake then swung both of her legs out toward the center of the room and slid her skirt a few inches up her thigh. "I'll let you see my panties if you don't tell her."

Uncle Don reached his right hand across the table, hooked the fingers of her left hand and gently pulled her to her feet in front of him, then raised up the front of her skirt. "I won't tell her that you let me see your panties, Becky," he said, visually examining her cotton triangle between her thighs. "But," he dropped her skirt and looked into her eyes. "I'm not so sure about the incident with Steve. She really ought to know about that, you know."

Becky's eyes grew large and her mouth was stuck open as she inhaled through it. She had been tricked.

"Of course, I could always give you a spanking here, and then it would remain our secret. But that's only if you want me to help you out."

There was a surge of warmth between Becky's legs. "Oh yes, please Uncle Don. Please, please let's keep it our secret." They had talked about secrets earlier.

"Then we had better go into the other room, we'll be much more comfortable on the couch." Uncle wrapped his right hand around her left wrist and led her down the hallway into the living room where he sat on the middle cushion and positioned Becky sideways on his lap. "Now then," he said, "First, tell me about Steve."

"Well, he's a year ahead of me and he's a really good student. He gets straight A's, even in math."

"And you like him?"

"Oh, yes." Becky looked down shyly. "He's very nice."

Uncle Don picked up her chin in the crook of his right index finger. "And that's the reason for letting him see up your skirt, then? Not the dollar?"

Becky vibrated her head up and down rather than answer. These questions made her feel so embarrassed but embarrassment in front of Uncle Don was an incredible turn on. Was it the scenario, his accent, a combination of the two or something else? She didn't care. She simply leaned against him, nuzzling his shirt in an attempt to hide her smile while uncle gave her a knowing hug, his left arm protectively around her. The idea of secrets with uncle was so naughtily erotic; her panties were already soaked, and he hadn't even touched her.

Uncle Don kissed the top of her head and whispered, "I think you'd better stand up and show me just what you did with Steve," then eased Becky to her feet facing him. "Don't you?"

"Yes, uncle," her immediate response came without thought. She looked down to see her hands had already clasped the front hem of her skirt, so she simply raised it until the damp front of her panties was completely exposed. There was the sudden realization that she really liked lifting up her skirt when he told her to.

Uncle leaned back as he studied her deliciously long legs. "Now tell me, did Steve just look?"

Becky bit at her lower lip. The secret relationship she was to have with Uncle Don required her to always tell him the truth. "Well, he wanted to touch me." Participating in this live story, saying these words, had turned her on more than she imagined possible.

"Like this?" Uncle leaned forward and brushed the back of his right index finger against her panties. The wet cotton pressed against her inflamed clitoris made her gasp audibly. He rested his finger against that perfect spot and looked up at her face. "Did you keep still when he pulled your panties down?"

"Yes...yes, please," she murmured through her trembling lips. She desperately wanted him to see how smooth she was, how she had shaved herself for him, just for him, just because he had told her to. Becky's profound desire for Uncle Don's approval had her almost begging for him to do whatever he wanted, just so she could hear the pleasure in his voice. She eagerly stepped out of her wet panties after he took them to her ankles and stood proudly, legs apart and skirt held high, giving uncle the absolute freedom to study her twitching vulva. The tip of his right index finger gently assessing her softness combined with his single word, "nice," pushed her over the edge. Her knees buckled but she slid into uncle's waiting arms. She had the muscle tone of a rag doll and Uncle Don effortlessly positioned his niece face down, prone across his lap with her feet at one end of the couch and her head resting on a pillow at the other. Becky felt her skirt being picked up and laid it across her back, exposing the pale flesh of her bottom, and held onto the pillow with both hands in delighted anticipation. She was already so aroused. So wet. The first few slaps were warm-ups and it was the tenth before she began to feel the heat, but by the twentieth she was panting and trying to spread her legs so her clitoris could make contact with something firm.

"Not yet," Uncle reprimanded, his hand pushing her legs back together, but after a few minutes she parted them again. She couldn't help it, she was writhing. Instead of another reprimand, however, Uncle simply shoved what might have been four fingers directly inside her. She gasped, she was almost there, but he removed them right away. "Keep still," he told her while massaging her tingling bottom with his soaked hand. She felt a tickle against her anus and instantly clenched it tightly, which earned her a quick swat across her right bottom cheek. The moisture made it sting. "I will touch you any way I wish and you will not resist. Do you understand?"

"Yes, Uncle Don," Becky gasped into the pillow, clutching it tightly to override her instincts as she felt a digit deliberately circle and then invade her butt. She exhaled and sank into the pillow, her hole quickly relaxing and accepting the slow in and out of what must have been Uncle Don's thumb. She was his to do with what he wished so, if he wanted to do this to her, then it was okay. She wasn't sure if she liked it or not but that didn't matter.

"There's a good girl."

She liked hearing that.

"And here's your good girl reward."

Four fingers were once again inside her with his thumb was still up her butt. Uncle slowly clenched while Becky tried to push up and arch her back, but his free hand between her shoulders held her down and all she could do was scream out repeated orgasms while his fingers played inside her. She came five times before her energy was depleted and then laid compliantly across her uncle's lap, panting.

"In this position, I have complete control over you." Uncle's voice had no point of origin, it was simply there. "I shall demonstrate. You will cum for me on the count of three."

She felt his fingers tighten as he counted out, "One, two," then a slight movement in conjunction with, "Three," took her once again over the top.

"Now I want you to try to resist," Uncle said calmly. "Try to control it, try not to cum when I order you to."

Becky gasped, tried to clear her mind and squeezed the hand that was so liberally using her with every muscle she could summon but, no matter what, she had no ability to prevent it and she came precisely when he commanded.

"You see," there was delight in his voice. "You have no control."

"Please," she whispered though irregular breaths. "Please, no more."

"No?" Uncle Don teased, but slowly removed his fist and caressed her crimson bottom, transferring the wetness from his hand to her, then rolled her over onto his lap and cuddled her.

"Did you like that?"

"It was incredible," she murmured, her body snuggling into him. "I never knew that was even possible." She had no thoughts of her own and basked in the sensation of simply being there in that moment. Her lack of control, his dominating her body to do as he wished, had so physically overwhelmed her that she was content to remain on his lap until her instructed her otherwise.

"You take well to spanking and being forced to orgasm." Uncle was nuzzling into her hair as he spoke softly.

"Whatever you want," she whispered back.

"Good girl." The praise in his voice conveyed his delight that Becky was beginning to understand her submissive role. "Now I'm going to strip you."

Uncle Don placed his hands around her bare waist and slid them up the sides of her torso, pushing her blouse upwards. She instinctively raised her arms and he pushed the blouse up and off her without unfastening the buttons. He hands fell naturally back across her breasts, but she instantly moved them down and to her sides to give uncle an unobstructed view.

"Stand up," he said, gently scooting her to her feet in front of him. He slid his hands up the sides of her legs, pushing her skirt up to once again admire her smoothness before unbuckling the waistband and letting the skirt fall to the floor. She stood proudly before him wearing nothing but shoes and socks, happily enjoying his clear pleasure with her body. He took her hands in his and rose in front of her. "Let's see how you do with my second criterion." He transferred her hands to his belt. "I want you to kneel for me."

Don's fingers gently toying with her hair was reassuring for Becky as she unbuckled his belt and unzipped his pants. Her eyes fixated on the eye level bulge in his black underwear as his trousers disappeared. She gingerly stroked it with two fingers from her right hand, it was firm and warm. Her whole hand then moved to caress him, her excitement overwhelming her anticipated trepidation of this moment. Her left hand joined in and she looked up for permission while massaging his balls and rigidity through the thin black cotton. Uncle nodded, perhaps he whispered for her to proceed but she wasn't sure. Regardless, she eagerly slid his underwear down and out of the way.

Becky had never seen an uncircumcised cock before but from what she read she knew that intact foreskin meant that the head of his penis was more sensitive than that of other men; if she performed correctly he would experience more pleasure from her than another man might. Doing so was no longer a means in order for him to continue to spank her; she wanted to give him that pleasure. Her left hand cradling the base of the shaft, she slid the foreskin back with her right while simultaneously opening her mouth and leaning forward to taste uncle's glistening purple bulb. It was not unpleasant. She pushed her tongue beneath it and sucked the first inch into her mouth while she closed her lips around it. She had been worried about not doing this correctly, it was important that Uncle Don be pleased with her, but when her eyes looked up at his and she was rewarded with his gaze of approval she relaxed and focused solely on being the best Becky she could be. Her tongue caressed the head of his cock while she began to gently rock her entire body back and forth, each time taking a little more of him into her mouth. With half of it now in and approaching the back of her tongue she remembered the popsicle analogy from that most instructive website she had found only days before and immediately began to suck. Uncle Don's cock took up more of her mouth and, afraid she might gag, she turned her head slightly so it would push up against the inside of her right cheek. Hands in her hair immediately corrected her faux pas. She was to be obliged to take him straight back. Her left-hand cradling uncle's balls, she tightly enveloped the lower half of his shaft with her right and began to slide up and down while vigorously sucking. Her lips were pounding into her hand, a perfect barrier against a gag reflex. She felt trembling inside her mouth and a sudden fear made her want to pull away, but Uncle Don's fingers entwined in her hair thankfully saved her from her instincts. He suddenly froze and the trembling in his cock gave way to a series of twitches and jerks as the hot semen flooded across the back of her tongue. She looked up at her uncle's face and, encouraged by the obvious ecstasy she was providing him, began rocking her head back and forth again while sliding her right hand away so she could take him in deeper. Becky's prior fears and inhibitions had disappeared, and she eagerly swallowed the cum in her mouth, continuing to suck and rock until Uncle Don's hands released her hair and she heard his approving, "Good girl."

"Did I do okay for you uncle?" Becky's eyes looked up pleadingly. Had she successfully met the criteria he had given her? Would he be willing to her be his Becky on an ongoing basis?

Her pussy still sensitive to even the slightest tough, Rebecca nervously undressed for bed that night. She and Nick had both enjoyed a much more satisfying, albeit still vanilla, sex life these past few weeks with a frequency that had increased to almost every night; being spanked had caused her to become more responsive to Nick's routine and, in return, he had been almost as affectionate with her as when they first met. Rebecca was in no way willing to upset this status quo. To ensure that Nick wouldn't see any facial grimace, Rebecca wrapped her arms around his neck as soon as he slid into bed and initiated a deep kiss while he pawed at her. Still locked in embrace, Nick rolled on top of his wife but instead of the anticipated pain Rebecca experienced an altogether different feeling as his excited cock slid between her still engorged labia lips and pressed her tingling bottom against the bed. In an animal embrace she gasped and wrapped her legs around him, squeezing as hard as she was able to force him deep inside her. To that spot that existed beyond the reach of Don's fingers. Bucking her hips in conjunction with her husband, Rebecca rediscovered the splendor of interactive sex, lost over so many years to the banality of married life. The resulting orgasm, simultaneous with Nick's expressive explosion, was by all means satisfying but nowhere near the intensity of that afternoon. Still, it did feel good and Nick actually held her for a few minutes afterwards and told her she was a wonderful wife before he rolled over and went to sleep.

"Wow!" Rebecca stared at the ceiling fan as she lay flat on the bed next to Nick's slumbering frame in contented contemplation. She felt complete. Now that Don had agreed to weekly sessions with her, Rebecca would be able enjoy her perfect married life without frustration and continue to be a better wife for Nick; all without having to cuckold him.

As Becky, she could experience the pleasures not afforded by married life at the hands of a gentleman who appeared to completely understand her, perhaps more than she understood herself. She completely trusted him. Don had awoken her submissive nature and, provided she continued to be a good girl for her uncle, he promised to help her to explore it more. She was so lucky to know such a generous man.

Rebecca pulled the blanket to her chin and snuggled into it as she rolled onto her left side, her semi sleepy mind remembering her perfect day as her eyes fluttered closed; the day she embarked on her journey to become a proper spankee.

6. Chapter Six: Implements

REBECCA STOOD AT DON'S front door and quickly unbuttoned her raincoat before ringing the doorbell; she wanted to ensure that Don would immediately see she was wearing the body-hugging silk dress that he had specified. "Brr, it's cold," he exclaimed as he held the door open, smiling at her as she scurried inside. He slid her out of the wet coat, hung it on a hook above the umbrella stand then stood behind her, his arms around her waist, and whispered, "I'd better fix you up with a cappuccino right away. Let's go to the kitchen."

Don said nothing about the items on the tabletop and calmly went to the center island to grind espresso beans while Rebecca slid onto a chair with her eyes fixated on them. She recognized the crop from before, but lying next to it was a flogger, stretched out to almost the entire width of the table, and a tan leather paddle. Her hands squirmed in her lap as she earnestly controlled her desire to reach out and touch these tools of such potential delight and discipline. Only a few days before she had sent Don an email confessing to watching online videos of women experiencing such things and sharing with him her curiosity of what it might feel like. She was ready for the pleasure pain of something more intense than spanking.

"Here you are, nice and hot." Don slid a mound of froth adorned with nutmeg and chocolate in an oversize cup and saucer in front of her, snapping her out of her pondering. She immediately picked it up with both hands while he added, nodding towards the items on the table, "I see you noticed the toys."

Rebecca's eyes widened as she peered at him over the cup. What a curiously flippant use of that word. She carefully put the cup back on the saucer while licking her top lip then coyly asked, "Will you tell me about them?"

"I would be delighted." Don put his cup down and picked up the paddle. "This is actually quite old," he said, tapping it gently into his open left palm. "It's made of a single piece of something called strapping leather, the same thing that a tawse used to be made of. In fact, if the striking end were cut into strips instead of being a single solid piece of leather it would be a tawse." He smiled. "Perhaps something down the road, eh? For now, though, it's important that you experience completely different types of implements, and a solid piece of leather is quite unique."

"What about that one?" Rebecca tried to conceal her excitement as she nodded towards the flogger.

"Ah, yes." Don put the paddle down on the table, stood up, then took the handle of the flogger in his right hand and slid the tails halfway over his left. "This, Rebecca, is a perfect flogger. These striking parts are called lashes and are made of hand cut deerskin." He held it out to her. "Feel how soft. Each lash is twenty inches long and there are thirty of them."

"They are soft." Rebecca was surprised that they weren't stiff as she had imagined. How could something so soft be effective for discipline?

Don gently pulled it back from her. "The weight of the handle equals the weight of the lashes, so it is perfectly balanced." He grinned. "Perfect balance means perfect control." He carefully laid it back down on the table and returned to his cappuccino. "Today we're going to have an exploratory session. I shall provide you with an introduction to each of these implements and we will then discuss them. Different people react differently to such things and so we need to find out which works the best for you." He drained his cup. "Tell me, are you concerned about marks?'

"Nick never looks at my butt." She picked up her drink. "I wish," she sighed. "I'm usually in bed first and we always keep the covers on. So no, no problem there at all," She smiled and quickly finished the beverage.

"Splendid." Don picked up the crop and pointed to a floor tile a few feet in front of where he was sitting. "Then we'll begin with you standing right there." He turned sideways in his chair as she moved into position and stood up straight with her hands behind her back. He overtly ogled her nipples straining through the bodice of the silk dress then slowly moved his eyes down to take in the shape of her legs against the fabric. "Panties?" he asked.

"Just the dress and sandals as you instructed, Sir."

"Show me."

Rebecca's hands went to her sides and she slowly gathered the dress up her legs until she was holding it at waist level, leaving her exposed and naked from navel to ankles. This pose of vulnerability was so much more erotic than being naked. It was so sensually submissive. She controlled her breathing and remained obediently still for Don's pleasure while he feasted his eyes on her milky thighs and her shaved-for-him pussy. Even when he slid from his seat and stood to the left side of her and, watching her face, administered six crisp swats to her naked bottom she remained both still and silent. "Good girl," he told her and pulled a chair away from the table. "Now that our friend the crop has provided you with a nice warm-up, you may bend over and place your hands on the seat of this chair. It's high time you met mister paddle."

Rebecca clutched the seat, her dress still around her waist, and braced for the impact of the paddle. Unlike the other implements, the pain and sound were simultaneous, and the first stroke caused her to claw her grip into the seat while she involuntarily cried out. The swat on the other cheek followed immediately and produced the same sounds. "Please, Sir," she blurted through her quivering mouth. "It hurts." Don had told her those were the words to use when she wanted him to ease off. She hung her head; glad to have stopped the paddle but now worried that she had disappointed Don. "I'm sorry," she murmured, afraid to look up. She felt Don's hands pry hers free from the chair and as he stood her up she lunged against him to bury her face in his shirt. His arms enveloped her and she felt his breath in her hair while his right hand soothed her bottom through the cool silk. "It's alright," he whispered, then kissed the top of her head.

Rebecca turned her moist eyes upwards. "You're not mad?"

"Of course not," He hugged her. "I told you that the purpose of today was to try out some implements and we have discovered that the paddle isn't your cup of tea." He slid his arms away and filled a glass with water from the dispenser on the front of the refrigerator. "Here, drink this."

Rebecca guzzled the water and smiled, "Thank you," as she returned the glass to him. Her gaze fell to the table. "Can we try the flogger?"

"Certainly," Don sat down and gently cradled the lashes into his left hand while his right gripped the handle. He looked up at her. "Strip."

That single word instantly made Rebecca forget about the two rectangular hot spots on her bottom and she pulled the dress up and over her head, anxious to once again have Don look at her. Anxious to enjoy the pleasure in his eyes as he did so. Her pussy twitched excitedly as she slid her hands behind her head and presented her naked torso to him.

"We can more fully appreciate the pleasures of the flogger if we sprawl you out on a bed." Don's English accent made the statement absolute. "Let's go upstairs."

Rebecca walked in front as they ascended the staircase. Don had never had her on a bed before. This was to be a new level of vulnerability, but she trusted him not to violate her hard limit or no vaginal sex.

"Lie face down," Don instructed, motioning towards the queen size bed ahead of them. "I want your legs apart and your arms above your head."

Rebecca squirmed into position and soon felt the gentle touch of soft leather against her shoulders. "Deerskin," Don reminded her, continuing the stroking motions down her back, all the way down the backs of her legs, then more towards the insides as he worked his way up again. It soothed her bottom and finished in upward glides against her arms. She then began to hear slapping sounds and her shoulder blades became warm. There was a tickle in the middle of her back, then more sound. Louder slaps preceded a flush of warmth across her buttocks, but this felt good. Frequency and intensity of the flogging to her behind increasing, she spread her legs in hopes that an errant lash might find its way between them, but all remained in Don's tight control. He deftly continued with his flogger to convert her entire bottom into a glowing furnace. Then, to put a halt to her attempts to grind her wanting pussy into the bed, he ordered her to flip over onto her back and keep still. Her legs spread; Don teased the insides of her thighs with the soft leather, admonishing her with a quick flip of his wrist to convert the soft stroke to a sting whenever she dared to flinch, until she had sufficiently demonstrated self-control.

"Much better," he said, and then treated her quivering vagina to the upward slide of the soft leather.

"Ohmygosh." Rebecca fought to close her mouth as her body arched in response.

"Open yourself up for me." Don calmly instructed. "Both hands."

Rebecca needed no encouragement. Her eager fingers immediately dove between her legs and pulled her labia lips apart, obediently presenting her all-too-ready clitoris for whatever he wished to do with it. It was less than a minute before the gentle dancing of the tips of the lashes delivered the hoped for reward, leaving her limp and panting on the bed while Don withdrew the flogger and placed it on the top of the adjacent dresser.

"You appeared to enjoy the flogger," Don teased Rebecca as she sat with a cold drink in the kitchen, her hot bottom enjoying the coolness of her silk dress. She smiled back demurely at his understatement and nodded affirmatively.

"But not the paddle," he added.

"They feel so different. The flogger is warming and stingy and I like that, but the paddle just hurts."

"Everyone is different, that's why it's so important to take the time to learn about implements before using them in a scene. That is, all except the cane."

Rebecca was intrigued. "You're not going to let me try out the cane?" She feigned a pout.

"No." Don slowly moved his head from side to side. "The cane belongs in the realm of the headmaster. If you wish to experience it you'll have to enter schoolgirl role-play and commit to receiving a minimum of six strokes."

Rebecca began to wriggle in her seat. She had watched women being caned on the internet videos and was already predisposed to trying it. The fact it was going to be Becky who was to be caned made it even more alluring. Rebecca very much liked being Becky and Don played the perfect headmaster to her schoolgirl. A cane was thin and nothing like a paddle so she wasn't worried; perhaps it would feel more like a crop. And six strokes didn't sound bad at all. She toyed at her lower lip with her teeth. Maybe if she liked it the headmaster would give her more than six.

"A cane also leaves marks," Don added. "Sometimes even welts, which might persist for several days."

Rebecca beamed at Don; his attempts to dissuade her were having the deliciously opposite effect. She often regretted how the marks from his spankings dissipated so rapidly but a caning carried with it the promise of reminders for days afterwards. She wanted it.

7. Chapter Seven: Headmaster

REBECCA WORE ONE OF Deborah's old school uniforms for authenticity. Now sporting a white cotton blouse and with naked knees between her pleated, plaid skirt and socks, she had transformed into schoolgirl Becky. She slowly walked down the hallway to the office where Don, in the role of the headmaster, would be waiting for her. Controlled breathing helped to alleviate some of the trepidation, but from her past experience with role-play she knew she would not be completely relaxed and in the moment until the scene actually began. She gingerly knocked on the door.

"Enter."

The headmaster was sitting behind his desk, clearly preoccupied with some sort of paperwork. At the click of the closing door the fingers of his right hand beckoned her to approach, but he did not look up until Becky was standing attentively in front of his large wooden desk. "Why are you here, girl," he asked her, his intimidating English accent sending a shiver down her spine, but also completing her transition into a schoolgirl.

"Mister Fordham sent me, Sir." Becky's clasped hands fidgeted behind her back. "He said I was to tell you I had been insubordinate."

"And, were you?"

"I'm afraid I must have been, Sir."

"This is not a charge to be taken lightly, young lady," the headmaster shook his head as he spoke. "Would you like to explain?"

"Well, it started with not having my homework done on time and ..."

The headmaster raised his right hand to silence her. "Stop your babbling girl and get to the point. What is it that you did that caused Mister Fordham to send you here?"

"I told him to 'chill out,' Sir." Becky gulped and eyes immediately fell to the floor. "I really didn't mean to." She felt the need to give an explanation but was having difficulty with appropriate wording. "It just sort of came out." Her voice faded away and she made a slight side to side movement with her head.

"Are you attempting to suggest that your lack of self-control might serve as justification for your atrocious behavior?" His English accent boomed incredulously.

Becky's head snapped up to attention. "No, not at all, Sir," She answered briskly.

"I should think not." He placed his hands flat on his desk and looked directly at her. "This is the second time I've seen you for this same offense, isn't it?"

"Yes, Sir," Becky replied meekly and looked down again. "It is."

"Then it is clear that spanking you did not prove sufficient to help you curb this unsavory tendency, did it?"

Becky gulped, hoping that question was rhetorical. It must have been, because the headmaster continued with, "Do you see that cane in the corner?"

Becky turned around and her eyes widened when she saw the bamboo rod leaning against the corner behind the door. It must have been three feet long. "Yes, sir." She swallowed hard.

"Bring it to me." He rose and stood by the side of the desk while Becky went to the corner and picked up the cane. It was so smooth, as if it had been polished. Fascinated, she ran the fingers of her right hand along it while she slowly walked back to the desk. From watching a cane being used in videos she had expected it to be bendy and pliable, yet in her hands it was a rigid rod, and that realization suddenly made her nervous about the upcoming punishment. She handed it to the headmaster who, with a flip of his wrist, caused it to produce the loud, whooshing sound that had so intrigued her.

"The cane is a splendid device," he told her. "Most instrumental is assisting errant young ladies, like you, to remember common courtesy towards their instructors." He tapped the back of one of the wooden chairs in front of the desk. "Bend over and put your hands on the armrests," he said nonchalantly.

This position had Becky bent over at ninety degrees, and as she clasped her hands onto the chair she felt a surge of excited embarrassment. Bending this way had pulled her skirt up in the back to where the headmaster could most likely see her panties. While she didn't dare to look over, she knew from where he was standing that was probably his intent. She was glad to be wearing the correct, regulation white cotton ones; the last thing she needed was a second infraction for incorrect attire. She tightened her grip as she felt her skirt being lifted and laid across her back. The headmaster made no comment about her panties other than to tell her he was obliged to pull them down in order to deliver her caning. She closed her eyes when she felt his hands at her waist and became conscious of her heart beating as he exposed her soft white buttocks. Slowly sliding her underwear down her legs, he left them around her ankles as if they were cotton shackles.

"You will receive six strokes." The headmaster was now standing to her left side, positioning the cane against her behind. "And you will count them out. Do you understand?"

"Yes, Sir," Becky replied instantly then bit nervously at her top lip. She had not expected a caning to be so participatory, thinking instead that she was going to be able to just keep still and quiet and take it. She braced herself.

The whoosh ended in a distinctive thud, just like in the videos, but the point of impact registered as instant band of hot spread evenly across both sides of her bottom. "One, Sir," she called out, just before the hot area began to sting and her breathing faltered. She was unable to recover her breath before the second swat landed and she sputtered an unrecognizable sound before being able to eke out, "Two, Sir."

The third stroke landed midway between the first two and somehow combined the stinging of the first two into a single glowing throb which rushed between her legs. "Three. Three Sir," she said with a gasp, her arms rigid and her head straining upwards. The next one fell lower, almost at the top of her thighs, and the burn teased her already inflamed pussy. She wanted to separate her legs, perhaps the next stroke might even brush up against her there, but the panties around her ankles prohibited it. Suddenly remembering, she blurted out, "Four, Sir." That act of speaking caused her to notice her lower jaw trembling and she became aware of tears forming in the corner of her eyes. Yet she was not aware of registering pain; the hot stings of the caning had aroused her to the point of disconnect.

Whoosh. The next sting was a little higher and her almost uncontrollable lower jaw made it hard to say, "Five, Sir. She tasted the salt of the tears running down her cheeks when she managed to force, "Six, Sir," out before she was no longer able to close her mouth and she stood facing the seat of the chair, panting, while drips from her chin splashed onto it. Her bottom stung and felt like fire, but her pussy was twitching uncontrollably and her legs were trembling. Thank goodness for the stability of the chair.

"I trust that you will now think twice before disrespecting authority." The headmaster, still holding the cane, leaned against the desk. "You may now stand up."

Becky pushed herself to an upright position and stood with her arms hanging by her sides.

"Pull your skirt up around your waist and hold that position. You will remain like that for five minutes of contemplation."

Becky's fingers scooped up the hem of her skirt and she compliantly pulled it around her waist, gathering it up in front of her with both hands holding onto it, very much aware of the headmaster looking at her. Was this part of the standard discipline or was he making her expose herself because he liked looking at her? She found herself hoping the latter. What was it about humiliation that could be so exciting, so erotic, for her? Her breathing was becoming rapid and shallow and she suddenly realized why: the index finger of her right hand, without any conscious input from her, had somehow found its way to her anxious clitoris. Her already unstable legs buckled but a quick move by the headmaster prevented her from tumbling to the floor. He held her up by her right arm. "You'd better lie down if you're going to do that, young lady," he told her, adding, "And get those panties off," as she tripped over them and stumbled towards him for support. Why is it that an English accent telling you to take your panties is almost enough to make you cum in and of itself? She pondered.

Becky offered no resistance as the headmaster maneuvered her to the desk and she obediently lay down on top of it while the he settled calmly into his leather chair. Even though the welts on her bottom were cushioned by her skirt, the pressure of this position was still stimulating them. It wasn't because she didn't care about the headmaster sitting there watching her; rather it was because of it that she so freely spread her legs and shoved both her hands between them. Eyes closed, Becky writhed and moaned with the same abandon as when she was alone until, satiated, she finally came to rest on her left side in contented exhaustion, the throbbing stripes across her buttocks shamelessly on full display.

Rebecca stood alone in her bathroom that night with her nightgown around her waist, a portable mirror in her hand and her back to the mirror above the sink, sporting a Cheshire cat grin as she studied the evenly spaced series of marks adorning her still red bottom.

She reached to touch them and just the act of running her fingers across the hot, raised flesh once again inflamed her wanting pussy as she recalled how she came by them. Hearing Nick enter the bedroom she quickly let go of her nightgown and put the mirror down to set about washing up. She wanted to turn the lights off and get into bed as soon as possible.

Suppressing a shocked sound as her bottom came in contact with the cold sheet Rebecca laid on her back with her arms at her sides and fought the urge to slide her fingers between her legs. Nick was taking forever to get ready for bed but, rather than disrupt their nightly routine by saying anything, she simply waited quietly until he joined her and ritualistically pushed up the front of her nightgown. He seemed pleased that he wasn't going to have to take time warming her up tonight and, not questioning her wetness, eagerly pounced on top of her. The pounding of the welts against the bed almost brought her to tears and, gasping, Rebecca clenched onto her husband through three pleasure pain orgasms before he exploded into her.

"You were nice and frisky tonight," Nick complimented as he rolled off her, then gave her a cursory kiss and proceeded to turn his back to her and instantly fall asleep. Rebecca remained still, happily panting until slumber overwhelmed her, and slept flat on her back for the entire night.

8. Chapter Eight: Daddy

"I HAVE A QUESTION ABOUT role playing." Rebecca twisted her mouth causing wrinkles to form on her forehead as she wrestled for a way to describe what had been bouncing around in her head since the caning session. She and Don were taking a daytime stroll through the park together, enjoying an unusually warm autumn day outside rather than sitting in the coffee shop. She sipped thoughtfully at her to-go beverage. "I really like the freedom of being Becky and I even think like a schoolgirl when I'm in that role. It's amazing but I really do become her."

"I've noticed; role play is definitely the ideal mechanism for you to explore your submissiveness."

"The problem I'm having, and please don't think I'm silly, is that, um, when I do something that I know a good girl shouldn't do I actually feel a bit ashamed." She looked cautiously at Don, but his understanding expression encouraged her to continue. "I mean, I like doing things and it's really a turn-on to have the headmaster look up my skirt and stuff and masturbating in front of him on the desktop was incredibly erotic. But afterwards I get worried about the headmaster's opinion of Becky, like he'd no longer see her as innocent and think of her as some sort of slut. Am I being weird?"

"Not at all," Don's response was instant and genuine as he shook his head. He was smiling from his hazel eyes, the blue green matching the colors in his tie. "Not only do I completely understand, but I can also provide you with a simple solution." He nodded towards a bench. "Let's sit down for a bit."

Rebecca sat attentively, hands clutching her drink in her lap. She dressed in regular street clothing for their weekly coffee chats and today was wearing a weather-appropriate pair of blue jeans and a sweater. When not in playtime mode they were to chat and interact as friends, but the fact that Don generally wore a business suit and always had the answer to whatever her question might be caused her to consistently see him as an authority figure. She wished she had worn a skirt. That was what Don liked. Why was it that whenever she followed even his simplest suggestion she instantly fell into submissive mode?

Don sat sideways at the other end of the bench and turned towards her. "All we have to do is create another role for you to play. Perhaps one in which you don't have a sense of what might be considered appropriate behavior."

"Ooo, I think I might like that." Rebecca bit at her lower lip but couldn't conceal the excitement from showing on her face. Her wide-open eyes gave that away. "Do I get to be a little girl with Uncle Don?"

Don's eyes had not left her while she spoke, and they continued to focus on her face while he took a long drink of his coffee. "I get the impression you've already given this some thought," he said, smiling as the effect of his words caused Rebecca to develop bright red elfin cheeks. She nodded vigorously then buried her face into her cup.

"Tell me about it," he nudged with parental calm.

"Well," Rebecca crossed her legs and twisted sideways towards Don. "I've watched some age play scenes online where the women are dressed up like little girls. They get to be completely innocent. They don't even care about whether you can see their panties or not, and their 'daddy' talks to them like little girls. You can tell they're really into the role play by the way they like the attention when he plays with them." She pulled her arms in towards herself and shrugged. "Can I have that?"

"But it's more than just playing though, isn't it? What happens if they have a temper tantrum or didn't want to do something that they were told to do?"

"Then daddy has to discipline them." Rebecca was starting to feel squirmy and realized that she had been fidgeting for the past several minutes.

"What sort of discipline?" Don wanted to give Rebecca every opportunity to describe exactly what she had in mind.

"Well, they first get told how they have misbehaved, and then daddy takes their clothes off them, and then they get spanked, and then daddy touches them to discipline them with his fingers. I watched one scene where a girl had three fingers pushed in. Wow." Rebecca grinned and blushed simultaneously. "But it always ends with her getting cuddled and daddy telling her she is his good girl."

"Next time, then," Don promised. He rose and put his hand out to help Rebecca to her feet. "We'll have an age play scene. I think I'll call you Babydoll."

Rebecca beamed. "Will it be okay if Babydoll calls you daddy?"

At Don's house that following Wednesday Rebecca scurried up the stairs and quickly turned the doorknob, anxious to enter the spare bedroom and see what clothing Don had laid out for her. Days of anticipation she had made her quite impatient to become Babydoll. There were two items on the bed. The first was a shift that could be described as either a long top or a very short dress. It was white, quite simple in design, but delicately embroidered with pastel flowers. Next to it was a pair of eyelet lace panties, which would have been incredibly sexy except for the fact they had frilly edges around the waist and leg holes. She grinned in delight and kept staring at them while she stripped out of her Rebecca clothing. Jewelry removed and completely naked, she slid the panties on and admired them in the mirror. There

was no question that these were 'little girl' panties, the frills assured
that, but the eyelets made them wildly erotic too. She picked up the
shift, dropped it over her head and then ran her fingers through her
long dark hair so it fell down her back. The 'dress' flared out from under
her arms and reached just to the top of her legs which left the lower
inch of the panties exposed. Now Babydoll, she posed in front of the
mirror and swayed from side to side, giggling at how readily the swishy
top flipped up to show off the frills. She heard the garage door open
and excitedly skipped downstairs to find greet 'daddy,' who had just run
out to pick up some ice cream.

"Hi Babydoll," Daddy greeted her and held up the bag from the
frozen custard store as he came back into the house. That was the best
type of ice cream; really squishy and soft. "Would you like sprinkles?"

"Ooo, yes please." She said, following daddy into the kitchen. The
tile was cold on her bare feet but she didn't mind. She watched daddy
put the carton on the center island and take a box of waffle cones and
a jar of sprinkles from the cupboard. "Oh, boy," she clapped her hands
together.

"Take those napkins," daddy nodded towards the table, "Into the
other room and put them on the coffee table. There's a special seat for
you in there."

Babydoll grabbed the stack of napkins and scooted down the
hallway into the living room. There was a huge pink beanbag chair next
to the coffee table and she immediately flopped into it. "This is so neat,
daddy," she called out. "Thank you." She then realized the napkins were
still in her hand and when she leaned forward to put them on the table
and had to spread her legs in order to maneuver in the chair. When
daddy came in carrying the cones, she was still sitting with her legs
apart and his affirmative expression told her that she was to continue
sitting that way.

"Here you are Babydoll," he said, handing her the cone that was
covered in colorful sprinkles then sat on the couch across from her.

"You'd better take a napkin so you don't make a mess." He picked one up and spread it across his lap.

"I'll be careful, daddy." Babydoll was eagerly licking at the custard which had already started to dribble down the side of the cone. Using her tongue to make designs with the sprinkles was as much fun as eating the ice cream, but frozen custard melts quickly and it was soon dribbling down her arm. Daddy got up, shaking his head, and left the room but quickly returned with two plates. He put his ice cream on one of them, took Babydoll's from her and put it on the other, then knelt next to her and used several napkins to wipe her arms. "Be careful," he warned as he returned her cone to her. "If you get any on your pretty dress, I'm going to have to spank you."

"Okay, I will," she responded perkily, and immediately resumed making swirls in the ice cream with her tongue. She knew daddy was watching her as she played more with the ice cream than eat it, rocking her body back and forth in the chair, happily oblivious to the melting confection. "Whoops," she suddenly called out as the cone slipped from her hand and landed on the front of her outfit. She looked up at daddy sheepishly. "I guess I should have used a napkin after all?"

Daddy scooped what he could onto the plate while Babydoll sat in the chair helplessly. He took more napkins and wiped up her arms and face, then told her to stand up as he slipped her shift up and off. He shook his head and pointed to the corner. "Kneel down over there facing the wall," he said, holding her top in his right hand. "I warned you twice to be careful, so you'd better take a few minutes to think about what has to happen now while I take care of this."

Babydoll knelt faced the wall as instructed and looked down; she was naked except for the frilly panties. Daddy was going to have to spank her now and just thinking about it was making her all tingly and squirmy. She sensed him return but didn't dare turn around and remained still and quiet until daddy took hold of her left wrist, pulled her to her feet and walked her to the couch.

"Your dress is in the wash," he told her as he sat on the couch and positioned her standing sideways in front of him. "Now, how many times did I tell you to be careful?"

'But I was being careful, daddy," she whined, slouching to her right side as she looked over at the plate on the coffee table. "Can if please finish my ice cream?"

A swift swat across her bottom was followed by daddy repeating the question.

"Umm, twice, daddy?" she winced.

"Twice I warned you, and you still refused to use a napkin." He shook his head. "And what did I tell you would happen if you got ice cream on your dress?"

"You'd spank me, daddy." Babydoll spoke softly but it was more because of growing excitement than trepidation. She began to sway from side to side in anticipation. Daddy held her left arm in his left hand and delivered six rapid slaps over her panties then, before she could catch her breath, pulled them down to her knees and effortlessly positioned her across his lap. Her bare bottom was just slightly red but sufficiently warmed up to take the solid stroke that accompanied the loud slapping sound without it stinging. But it felt good. Daddy quickly increased the intensity of the spanking, though, and after just a couple more she felt a wild combination of heat and pain and tingles. The seventh slap had her panting and her mouth began to quiver. She was so turned on. So ready. All she needed was a simple touch her between her legs. She squirmed, hoping to make daddy realize her need, but instead he stopped and pulled her back to her feet and slid her panties back up. What was going on?

"Okay, Babydoll. Let's try again." Daddy picked up the plate with her half-melted ice cream on it and a spoon. "Now that you've been reminded, perhaps you'll be able to finish your ice cream without making any more mess," he told her. "Sit down."

A frustrated Babydoll plopped into the beanbag chair and the cold vinyl exacerbated her already aroused bottom. She reached out and took the plate, but before daddy had returned to the couch she let it slip from her hands and land upside down in her lap. "Oops," she said, more jovially than apologetic.

Daddy was instantly as her side and Babydoll sat silently with her legs spread while he cleaned up the mess between them. The combination of his touch and the creamy melting ice cream which had soaked her panties was incredible.

"I'm not buying that as an accident," daddy said with a matter-of-fact tone as he put the plate down on the table. "But there's one sure way to deal with spoiled little girls." He put his hands on his hips as she lay in the beanbag chair semi-smiling up at him. "That's right," he nodded. "You're going to receive a real disciplining now. Turn over."

Babydoll rolled over and laid flat across the beanbag chair, gripping onto it as daddy slid her wet panties across her hot bottom and pulled them off. She tried to grind her twitching pussy into the chair but didn't have enough body control in this position to make it effective. Daddy knelt next to the chair and gathered her wrists together in his left hand, further adding to her helplessness, and delivered two tear inducing swats, one to each bottom cheek. "Oww," she cried out loudly, but daddy ignored her and all she could do to protest was move her head from side to side while two more hard slaps followed. She began to blubber and daddy rolled her over on her back, causing her blubbers to become gasps as the cold contacted her blazing flesh. While her wrists were still held above her head, Babydoll was now able to put her feet on the floor and that stability enabled her to squirm and gyrate. "Please, daddy," she begged. "Please touch me."

"You're here for discipline," daddy reminded her with a sadistic smile, but then shoved two, then three, fingers into her soaked pussy. There was no resistance. He turned his hand to align his fingers against her g-spot while his thumb pressed onto her clitoris, and then leaned onto her to hold her down as she tried to arch her back in the resulting ecstasy. The throes of orgasm subsided after a minute and Babydoll gave daddy a thank-you smile. But he wasn't finished with her. "Now we have that out of the way," he said, "We can proceed with teaching you what happens to naughty girls who have temper tantrums."

Babydoll felt daddy's fingers ram further inside her, forcing her even more open. She involuntarily produced a myriad of strange sounds as his fingers explored and gave her sensations she had never known before. She tried to fight against his grip, but he was too strong. Was that a fourth finger going inside her now? She suddenly screamed but didn't know if it was in pain or delight. Then, suddenly, she felt strangely comfortable with his hand in her. "That's right," he assured her. "You will now do as I tell you. I'm going to count to three."

Babydoll felt his fingers moving inside her and, when daddy announced, "Three," she bellowed as her body convulsed into an intense forced orgasm. "No more," she gasped. "I'll be good."

"I'll decide when discipline is over," daddy calmly told her. "But if you feel you have a say in the matter, then you should refuse to cum when I command. Try it now. One, two..."

Babydoll screamed as her body once again lost control to daddy's count of three. "I can't," she panted. "Please...."

"One more should do it," daddy told her. "So, let's make it a good one."

Babydoll could offer no resistance as daddy's fingers began to clench inside her for the final time and her last drops of energy were spent on uncontrollable shuddering. Even after daddy released her she remained limp, lying in the beanbag chair drenched and completely spent until he picked her up, wrapped her in a huge fluffy pink towel and carried her to the couch. Sitting on daddy's lap, Babydoll happily snuggled against his warm strength while he cuddled and soothed her for the most contentedly disconnected hour she had ever experienced.

9. Chapter Nine: Masochism

IT WAS A HOT CHOCOLATE Friday and Rebecca and Don sat at the table next to the picture window in their favorite coffee shop enjoying steaming mugs with the cold rain pounding the pavement outside. Rebecca's had whipped cream on top and she delighted in licking her top lip after each slurp. "So tell me," Don peered at her across his mug as he spoke. "What did you think of being Babydoll?"

"It was an absolutely fantastic session, but I have a question. How come you only spanked Babydoll before fingering her?" Rebecca looked at Don quizzically. "I thought when you said discipline that meant you were going to start introducing, um, 'implements'?" She spoke freely because the inclement weather had not only kept other customers away and they were the only patrons in the coffee shop, but the pounding of the rain outside would also drown out their voices.

"Implements would be out of the bounds of age play. The 'youngest' girl that would have an implement used would be a cane on a schoolgirl."

"I see," Rebecca smirked. "So there's actually a hierarchy of discipline?"

"Indeed, there is. Spanking, of course, is across the board, but role playing provides a potential spankee the ability to define the extent of additional forms of discipline." He took a long drink of his hot chocolate while Rebecca absorbed his words before adding, "And in your case, the ability to disconnect and assume another identity."

"Is oral not allowed for Babydoll either, then?" Rebecca's coy smile was the closest she had ever come to admitting she thoroughly enjoyed performing this way for Don. She had expected, and really wanted, to do it as Babydoll.

"Absolutely not," Don feigned shock and put his cup down. "At least, not with 'daddy,'" he added with a smirk, but then composed himself. "My interpretation of a daddy is purely a disciplinarian."

"Well, I can tell you that I certainly enjoyed that discipline." She wrinkled her mouth and turned to look out of the window. "Would the headmaster ever finger a student like that?" Her eyes returned to Don. It was the question that Rebecca had been toying with for days and she had finally developed enough courage to blurt it out. Her recurrent fantasy of being caned again had expanded since her session as Babydoll and it had become so pervasive a fantasy that she simply had to share it with Don. She was willing to make whatever deal he wanted if he would do that for her, open to even discussing her hard limit if that was what is was going to take. The fact he never brought the subject of vaginal intercourse up continued to emphasize that Don was a true gentleman and fully deserving of her trust, but this forbidden fruit had also begun to enter her fantasy dreams on more than one occasion.

"Other than for spanking, the headmaster doesn't touch the students. Discipline of that sort belongs at home." Don clearly understood what Rebecca wanted but he was going to make her say it. Earn it. "Don't you like the way daddy fingers Babydoll?" he teased.

"Oh, I love it." Rebecca blushed and looked away again. "But Babydoll only gets spanked and I, um," she turned back. "I want to see what it would be like to be fingered to orgasm right after being caned," she mumbled, eyes looking up.

"I see." Don was enjoying this. "And since only the headmaster does caning you want schoolgirl Becky to also be fingered by him."

"Um hmm," Rebecca nodded enthusiastically but her pursed lips were a bit too embarrassed to speak.

"Well then." Don finished his drink, deliberately put his mug down and sat back with his hands flat on the table. "The only way that could come about would be if Becky initiated an impropriety." Don's grin expanded to show his teeth. "If she came across as some sort of a slut it would free the headmaster's sadistic side and he might be willing to make a deal."

Rebecca contained her excitement by focusing on her cup and instead of yelling out, "Anything you want," she managed to calmly ask, "What sort of a deal?"

"Offer to swallow instead of being caned," Don responded as if it was an intuitively obvious answer. "Most likely, Becky will then get both."

Rebecca looked thoughtful, raised her mug to her lips and slowly finished her hot chocolate. Don was cool and calm, so why were his words so hot? She crossed her legs under the table to stop her thighs from rubbing together as her froth covered lips emerged from the rim of the mug. "Deal," she said, before licking them clean.

Becky stood attentively in the familiar position in front of the headmaster's desk. Legs together, hands behind her back and looking down, she listened to his broad accent berating her atrocious behavior with matter-of-fact lack of inflection. Yet in spite of his always controlled demeanor it was obvious that he enjoyed looking at her. Her schoolgirl uniform was perfectly designed for such nefarious purposes; seemingly innocent but comprised of a blouse that clearly outlined her breasts and a pleated skirt that was so easily lifted up. Surely, he desired more than to just look at her. Today she was determined to have him reveal those base instincts. Yes, she wanted to be caned again, and she desperately needed for the headmaster to take control of her body and render her to his mercy; this was the fantasy that had led to this scene. But her ultimate desire was to satisfy a need that she couldn't explain; her need to know that she had pleased him.

"Are you listening to me, young lady?"

"Yes, Sir," Becky responded instantly. "I am to receive a double punishment for my continuing to be disrespectful to my teachers, sir."

"Let's hope that two sets of six will serve as a more lasting reminder this time."

"May I ask a question, Sir?" Becky had thought long about how she was going to broach this.

"You may."

"I understand the need for a double punishment, Sir, but might the second one be, um, something other than a caning?"

"What is it that you have in mind, girl?"

"If it pleases you, Sir, you could finger me and discipline me that way if you want to." She bit at her top lip and looked at the floor.

"You little guttersnipe." The headmaster rose to his feet and looked down at her across his desk. "And what, pray tell, makes you think I would want to do something like that?"

"Because I'd suck your cock and never tell anyone about it, Sir." They were incredibly hard words to say but, once out, Becky was flush with a combination of relief and excitement. She had actually said it.

The headmaster walked slowly to the corner of the room, picked up the cane and pointed it towards her. "You realize I should have you expelled for that, don't you?"

Becky gulped and remained rigid; she had no words.

"But if I were to acquiesce to your offer of impropriety, you do realize that it would have to be on my terms, don't you?"

"Yes, Sir," Becky responded with relief in her voice.

"Very well," he nodded affirmatively and brandishing the cane in his right hand tapped it on the back of a chair. "Bend over."

Becky leaned over and gripped the wooden arms while the headmaster laid her skirt across her back. She closed her eyes as she felt his hands slide around her exposed waist and gasped silently as he slipped them inside her panties to feel her before pushing them all the way down to her ankles. Her pussy was already twitching before the first stoke of the cane even made contact with her bottom. By the time the third one struck she was breathing heavily through her wide-open mouth, desperate for relief. Her bottom burned, she might have been crying, but all she could think about was the headmaster shoving his fingers into her after the caning was over. When she finally blubbered out, "Six," quickly followed with a panting, "Sir," it took all of her remaining strength to continue to hold her trembling body in place. The cane tapped against her right calf and she instinctively raised her foot and it was suddenly free from the panties around it.

"Legs apart, young lady."

Becky obediently spread her legs, planting her feet eighteen inches apart and clutched the chair even tighter as she felt the headmaster's hands caress her glowing buttocks. His touch simultaneously inflamed and soothed the emerging welts and his deftly placed thumbs on each side of her labia lips increased her arousal as the fire from her bottom consumed her wanton pussy. She shuddered to orgasm the instant his fingers entered her, three in a single movement, but then they were out again. Moisture was trickling down her legs.

"You will now receive the disciplining you requested," the headmaster said calmly and roughly shoved four fingers all the way inside her. Becky's knees buckled and her head went up but the headmaster's free hand simply pushed down on the back of her neck and she locked back into position. The movement of four fingers quickly brought about a second orgasm but the headmaster appeared to ignore it in favor of continuing to expand her, open her up more. "We're almost there," he announced as if speaking to an impatient child.

Becky suddenly screamed in what could only be described as ecstatic pain as the headmaster's thumb slipped inside and he twisted his hand in order to push it against her g-spot while his fingertips found a deeper contact. Her whole body shook as hot liquid gushed across the headmaster's hand and flowed down her trembling thighs. "That's three, Sir," she gasped through her tears.

"We will continue until you verbally repeat your offer," the headmaster advised, adding, "and include that you want to take it to completion."

Becky's body somehow continued to hold onto the chair through the fourth orgasm while she tried to formulate the necessary words to end the fisting. "Wait," she panted as she felt his fingers begin to once again tense. "Please. Please, Sir." She was going to have to say it in one breath. "Please cum in my mouth, sir."

Her own words pushed her over the edge but this time the headmaster slowly removed his hand and allowed her to crumple onto the floor. When she looked up, he had already unfastened his pants and she was greeted by his rigid eight inches within licking distance of her mouth. Becky compliantly parted her lips as he pulled back the foreskin to reveal the glistening, purple head and she leaned forwards to take it in. The headmaster grabbed her head with both hands and, his fingers entwined in her hair, he forced his already pulsing cock directly to the back of her tongue. She closed her mouth around him and sucked, but it was clear that he was going to take his pleasure from her rather than permit her to give it. Her arms remained limp by her sides and she offered no resistance as she desperately tried not to choke while the headmaster pumped in an out with selfish abandon. He was fucking her mouth. Why did she like it so much? Why did she nearly cum the instant he told her that he was going to make her swallow?

Completion didn't take long, and Becky was soon submissively gulping and sucking hot semen from the headmasters throbbing rod. She felt an overwhelmingly strange sense of contentment in doing so, relishing in his moans of delight and happily continuing to suck his cock long after the pulsing has subsided, until he withdrew it from her.

10. Chapter Ten: Flogger

"I'M VERY ENCOURAGED by your progress, Rebecca," Don said as he handed Rebecca a glass of white wine and settled onto the couch next to her. Their email correspondence in the past five days since the caning/fisting session had been most prolific, with her expressing both how shocked she was that she enjoyed the rawness of the scene so much and her desire for more like it. She also wanted to include other forms of discipline; specifically, a session which included the flogger. "I believe that role playing may have served its purpose for you," he added. "So it's now time for you to realize your desires as a fully engaged adult." This was the culmination of a series of emails dealing with how comfortable Rebecca had become with Don and how she was now able to separate spankee Rebecca from real world Rebecca; no longer needing to adopt another persona. Don had told her that, as an adult, she would be entitled to a complete array of spanking and associated implements and her need for this had diminished any residual guilt she may have harbored to the depths of insignificance.

Rebecca turned sideways to face him, sliding her right leg up onto the couch to brazenly provide him with a view of naked thigh above her black stocking while she took a sip of her wine. She had worn a dark, form-fitting dress for this afternoon meeting at Don's house, nicely complementing his pinstriped business suit and tie. "No more cute outfits?" she asked.

"Oh, we're keeping the outfits." Don moved his eyes from unapologetically looking up her dress to join her in a smile. "But now we have a working knowledge of what it is that you like you'll have no more need for daddy or the headmaster. It's time for our spanking relationship to move to the next phase."

Rebecca liked the sound of that.

"I couldn't help but notice that the headmaster seemed to unleash a masochistic streak in you." Don took a swig of his wine. "What are your thoughts about that?"

"It's more than you realize." Rebecca's mouth contorted uncontrollably and she wrested it down to a simple smirk. "It was so hot having to ask," She took a gulp of wine. "But I think it would be even hotter to, um, you know, be forced to." Her eyes widened. She was shocked at how easily she had shared that sentiment.

"I'm confident that can be arranged."

"Maybe, you could tell me what you're going to do to me?" Rebecca's face was beaming, this was a wonderful conversation. "Right before you, um, you do it?"

Don was slowly nodding affirmatively. He understood completely. "What do you know about bondage?" he asked. "It might fit nicely into the type of scenes you're describing."

"Then I'd be completely at your mercy, wouldn't I?" Rebecca leaned further back on the couch and afforded Don a clear view of the fact she was not wearing panties. "But what else would you do with me? Will you want to take me in other ways?"

"Perhaps," Don replied thoughtfully while clearly enjoying his vantage position. "But you never have to worry about your hard limit." He guzzled the last of his wine. "That remains inviolate."

Rebecca sipped at her wine, pondering what 'other ways' might entail, and watched Don as he put his glass down and reached over the side of the couch, but then she immediately drained it and cleared her mind when he produced the flogger.

"Stand up," he said and flopped the lashes onto his open left palm. "Stand up and take off your dress for me."

Rebecca eagerly rose to her feet and, facing Don, slowly unfastened the top button on her dress. By the time she had reached the third one it was clear that she was not wearing a bra, but it wasn't until the last button was undone and she seductively slid out of the dress that Don was able to see the excitement in her nipples. She stood erect, wearing only stockings and heels, and dropped the dress onto the couch. "Like this?" She asked sweetly.

"Exactly like that," Don responded, eyes fixed on her. He stood up and, crop hanging from his right hand, walked towards her. "And now I want you to bend over the back of the couch."

The cold leather against Rebecca's flesh caused her to flinch but she overcame the feeling by pressing into it, warming it with her body. Firmly supported in this position with her feet slightly separated and her palms flat on the cushion, her bare bottom was deliciously exposed and vulnerable, ready to take the flogger. She closed her eyes in anticipation.

"There are two ways to use a flogger," Don explained. "The correct way is with a whole arm movement, like this."

Rebecca heard a thud and suddenly her whole bottom was hot. Three more thuds followed, and the heat covered not only her buttocks but also the tops of her legs and was rapidly spreading between them.

"The second way is to use wrist action," Don continued as if her were conducting an instructional lecture. "This is typically not advisable because the weight of the flogger can cause torsion in the wrist but, if you know how, it can provide a much more specific sensation. I'll demonstrate."

The feeling was, indeed, different as the tips of the lashes stung the insides of her thighs, only inches away from her twitching pussy. Rebecca tried to slide her feet further apart, but the height of the couch back prevented her from spreading sufficiently to permit the flogger to make erogenous contact.

"And now we'll mix it up." Don proceeded to deliver a continuous flogging from different angles and varying levels of intensity, causing Rebecca to begin to bounce slightly with each stroke. It was hot and wonderful. While the flogger was concentrated on her hind section, her nipples were stimulated with each stroke as they were forcibly rubbed against the leather and each lash landing make her pussy flinch. Her whole body afire, she moaned and writhed with her hands jumping from the seat to slap against the back of the couch as she tried in vain to grind her labia lips against it.

"That might just do it," Don announced in response to her clear loss of control. He placed the flogger across the back of the couch and eased a trembling Rebecca to her feet, holding her against his body to prevent her from falling. He engulfed her shoulders in his left arm and whispered into her hair, "I'm going to tie your hands behind your back now."

Rebecca watched wide-eyed as Don removed his necktie with one hand, then released her to lean against the couch as he tied one end of his tie around her left wrist. He quickly flipped her around and in what seemed like an instant her wrists were bound together behind her back and she was once again in the embrace of his left arm. He pulled her close and watched her mouth gasp as his fingers alighted on her clitoris and began to vibrate. She came almost immediately, eyes happily gazing into his as her shuddering legs gave way and he eased her to her knees in front of him. "I'm going to cum in your mouth now," He told her. "And you're going to swallow every drop."

Helpless and aroused beyond belief, she opened her mouth as he grabbed her head with his left hand and pushed the head of his cock between her lips. His right hand was around his shaft which meant she only had a couple of inches of him in her mouth. "Suck and massage it with your tongue," He ordered, stimulating himself as she compliantly obeyed. His grip on her hair tightened as his hand moved faster and faster and the bulbous head of his cock grew larger in her mouth until he suddenly froze with an ecstatic moan and hot cum flooded across the back of her tongue. Panting, he eased his grip and then rocked back and forth, sliding his cock in and out of her mouth while she swallowed. All the time her eyes were looking up at him adoringly.

Rebecca happily drifted off to sleep that night. She had many questions but trusted Don to provide all of the answers when he decided she was ready. He promised to properly tie her up so she couldn't move and flog her next time; she could hardly wait. She knew her dream that night would likely include him, causing her to ponder more as she entered the semi-conscious pre-sleep state about what he meant when he said he would take her in other ways, yet not violate her hard limit. Whatever it was, it was going to be okay with her.

11. Chapter Eleven: Restraints

"I THINK YOU MAY HAVE me addicted to cappuccino," Rebecca spoke as soon as the high-pitched squeal of steaming subsided. She watched Don pour the freshly created froth from the small silver pitcher over the aromatic espresso, adding, "Along with the other things you do," with a smirk. Friday morning coffee in Don's kitchen was so much more relaxed than at the coffee shop. Instead of sitting with her feet under the table as she would have done there, she was sideways on the tall chair with the heel of her right shoe teasingly perched over the crossbar while the left hung down towards the tile floor. Her arms secure around the backrest, she leaned back and seductively swayed from side to side to provide Don with visual access to the black panties she was wearing under her blue silk dress while he stood at the center island preparing their drinks. His smile of approval gave her a warm glow.

"Since we're not role playing today," she said, "I thought you might like it if I wore grown up panties for you." Although Rebecca had consciously refrained from using the word 'sexy' she was desperately hoping he would view them in that way. Why was it so important to her that Don should view her as sexually desirable when she had a hard limit of no vaginal intercourse in place? Could she be waffling on her resolve? Perhaps she would cave if he asked her, but Don would never ask; he was the epitome of a man-of-his-word and that discussion had already been had. Still, that was quite some time ago.

"And are you wearing a matching bra?" Don's response shook her from her musing. He added the finishing sprinkles of chocolate and nutmeg and carried the cappuccinos to the table while Rebecca sat up straight and unfastened the top two buttons of her dress.

"But of course," she answered, grinning as she pulled the silk back to reveal her black lace adorned breasts. "I know the rules."

"Very good; and I like your choice of black for non-age play. It makes a nice contrast." Don took a sip of his drink and teasingly added, "Black also matches the restraints I'm going to introduce you to."

For these past months Rebecca had explored her need to be spanked by assuming an alternate identity and entering into role play scenarios. It was so very easy to bend over and do as she was told while in the persona of a young girl with a trusted authority figure and Don, playing the roles of both trusted uncle and sadistic headmaster, had introduced her to something new every time he pulled down her little girl panties. Now, having learned to accept her desires rather than try to hide from them, she had entered a new phase; that of being spanked as an adult, the person she actually was.

Rebecca's eyes peered large over the oversize cup and she slowly lowered it to reveal her froth covered smile. As her trust in Don had grown so had her desire for more intense attention from him, but her involuntary reactions to his hard spankings and expert use of implements was preventing her from challenging the limits of her tolerance and was keeping those limits artificially low. Lower than what she wanted and far below what she now knew she needed. It was through bondage that she was going to be able to override these annoying tendencies of hers that were standing in the way of achieving the promise of pleasure-pain ecstasy she so desperately wanted Don to deliver. Today was to be her introductory session into the world of bondage spanking. She drained her cup. "May I see them?"

"Certainly, they're on the coffee table." Don smiled as they both slid to their feet and stood facing each other. "But you'll have to leave your dress here before we go into the living room," he said, tapping the back of her chair.

Rebecca obligingly unfastened the rest of the buttons, seductively removed her dress and, after sliding it over the chair, stood attentively mere inches away from him with her hands behind her back, eagerly awaiting his next instruction. Don gently stroked her left cheek with the backs of the fingers of his right hand then traced a line with his fingertips down the side of her neck and along the top of her bra. "Ready?" He whispered rhetorically as his hand slipped back across her breasts and latched around her left wrist, ready to lead her into the living room.

Rebecca's fluctuating facial expressions revealed her confused, almost overwhelming, mix of excitement and trepidation as her widening eyes alighted onto the objects on the coffee table. Five black restraints, each with two rows of silver studs and silver buckles with clasps, were laid out in a row. One was longer than the others, presumably it was a collar? Lying next to them was a black leather flogger and at the other end of the table was a black riding crop. Don stood behind her, his hands just off her shoulders and whispered into her left ear that she should sit down next to him on the couch.

"We'll begin with the wristbands," Don said, reaching across the table and picking up the two shortest restraints. Rebecca watched as he buckled them onto her wrists and bit her lower lip as he turned her away from him and clasped them together behind her back. He silently then picked up the longer restraint and, after indicating for her to lean her head forward, pushed her raven locks out of the way and buckled the collar around her neck. "Stand up," He ordered, easing Rebecca to her feet and placing her facing him with her feet eighteen inches apart. Don reached for the crop and began to lightly tap the inside of her right thigh, then gave equal time to her left. There was always a balance to his ministrations. Rebecca suppressed the urge to moan when Don began to rub the small rectangular leather end against the front of her panties but the fact she pushed against it didn't escape him and resulted in earning her three quick taps there instead as Don flicked his wrist.

"Turn around," he instructed. "We can't be ignoring your bottom."

The audible slapping sounds as the crop made repeated contact on the skin just below the leg bands of Rebecca's panties were accompanied by light stings. Don was beginning lightly; teasing her. She then felt the back of her panties bunched together as if they were a thong and pulled up as Don rose from the couch and provided each buttock with half a dozen non-teasing strokes. Standing still, standing at all, was suddenly Rebecca's greatest challenge. Don turned her back around, sat down in front of her and ran his hands up the outsides of her legs. "We're just warming you up," he announced jovially and, while looking up at her face, proceeded to pull her already soaked panties down to her knees. Rebecca for the first time realized the helplessness brought about by having her hands tied behind her back as Don eased her over his lap; she was completely dependent upon him not to drop her. She liked that feeling, the trust. She snuggled the left side of her face against the seat of the leather couch while Don placed her legs on the other side of him so she was fully laying the length of the couch, her naked bottom raised up over his strong thighs as he sat in the middle, her arms immobilized behind her back.

Since Rebecca's bottom was previously warmed by the crop Don began her spanking with more intensity than usual. She gasped and tried to raise her head, but Don took hold of the metal ring attached to the collar and simply kept his left hand down on the couch causing her face to remain in position against it. "You're now experiencing the beauty of restraint," he said as he calmly continued spanking her progressively glowing behind. Rebecca's audible, open mouthed breathing became grunts, and when it became clear to Don that she was straining against the panties around her knees in a feeble attempt to separate her legs, he switched from spanking her bottom to massaging it. Rebecca's labia lips were twitching wildly but she could neither touch her clitoris nor move into a position to rub it against something; Don's leg, the couch, anything at all would have done the job. Don squeezed her flaming buttocks, intensifying Rebecca's need and causing her to tighten her muscles even more against the restraints. The more she strained, the hotter she became. Don slid his hand between her legs, effortlessly entering her with what must have been four fingers but withdrew them before she could buck against them. He then used her ample moisture to further massage her bottom. "I believe it might now be time for the flogger," he told her.

With a single movement, Rebecca's panties slid past her feet and were gone. Don unsnapped her hands and rubbed each of her arms awake, then instructed her to stand up, walk over to the table and kneel in front of it. Hands now free, Rebecca fought against the almost uncontrollable urge to rub her quivering pussy as she stood up, planning to do so discreetly as soon as she was kneeling. But Don ordered her to put her hands on the top of the table before she was able to touch herself. Standing behind her, Don's feet pushed her knees apart and he unfastened and removed her bra. Still panting, Rebecca watched him attach ropes to each of the wrist restraints and wondered how long she would be able to remain at this intense edge of orgasm without falling over it. Was it possible to achieve a climax without being touched?

"Lie down across the table, reach up as far as you can and grab the sides," Don said with his authoritatively English accent. The tabletop was cold against her breasts, a stark contrast to the heat she was feeling from the waist down, and she grasped the table tightly to help offset the need to gasp out. Chin on the tabletop, Rebecca watched Don tie the other ends of the ropes to the legs of the table and she was once again restrained. "It's flogging time," Don quipped as he stood up and disappeared somewhere behind her. It seemed only an instant, though, before she felt the soft tails of the flogger sliding across her shoulders. "One day you may want a full flogging," Don teased, "To include your shoulders and upper back as well as your bottom and thighs." The tails were sliding down her back and a quiver of anticipation vibrated up Rebecca's spine. "But since your interest is currently just that of a spankee, we shall confine your flogging to..."

Whoomph, the full weight of the tails fell evenly across Rebecca's entire bottom. Why did that feel so good? Three successive strokes fell in the same manner, but Rebecca only interpreted them as increasing heat, increasing desire. The sensual leather proceeded to striking the backs of her thighs, and then to the tender inside portions. Needing to arch her back against the wave of pain Rebecca pulled against the wrist restraints with all she could muster. Although they didn't budge, her futile fight offset the pain or, more accurately, converted it. Into what, she had no idea. But, instead of registering pain she suddenly realized she had spread her knees as far apart as she could in a desperate attempt to get her pussy closer to the striking flogger.

"You like mister flogger, I can tell." Don's voice was suddenly all around her and the flogging had stopped. She felt something brush against her labia; Don was swinging the flogger back and forth between her legs. "See," he added as she tried to wriggle her bottom so the strokes might fall onto her clitoris.

"Please," Rebecca pleaded. Surely, he would touch her now. She had never been this close for this long.

Don moved to the other end of the table and untied her right wristband, but then immediately clipped it to the ring on the collar around her neck. "We can't have you losing control and touching yourself now, can we?" he said, reading her mind while repeating the activity on the other wrist.

Don eased her to an upright kneeling position on the floor, but before she was able to squeeze her legs together, he assisted her up and told her to sit on the table. "Scoot back," he ordered, "So your knees are at the edge."

The cold table against Rebecca's flaming bottom and thighs made her inhale more than she would have imagined possible through her wide-open mouth and transported her into an unfamiliar dreamlike state. Don raised her legs and effortlessly caused her to lie on her back. Feet now pointing at the ceiling, her bottom was freed from contact with the table. Her body had been converted to gelatinous quivering mass and her voice no longer worked. Her hands, secured at her neck, were vibrating against her face. Holding her ankles up and together with his left hand, Don deftly positioned the index and middle fingers of his right to deliver the coup de grace to Rebecca's delicious agony. She had never before screamed so loudly nor writhed so uncontrollably as Don's fingers danced on top of her engorged clitoris All that existed for her was the sensation of that moment.

When she recovered, Rebecca was naked and curled up in Don's embrace on the couch with no recollection of how she got there or when the restraints had been removed. Her voice restored, she simply exhaled, "Wow," and contentedly cuddled against Don's torso while he toyed with her disheveled locks.

"Do you have any idea of the time?" Don asked her.

"None," she giggled and fluttered her eyebrows. "Is it lunchtime, maybe?"

"More like afternoon tea."

"You're kidding!" Rebecca turned to strain at the mantelpiece clock. It was, indeed, almost four o' clock in the afternoon. "Wow," she repeated.

12. Chapter Twelve: The Edge

ALONE IN HER BATHROOM the next morning, Rebecca's face transitioned from an involuntary smirk to delighted laugher as she examined the marks still remaining on her bottom. Don had promised to give her introduction to bondage spanking and yesterday had certainly been one hell of an introduction. As she expected, instead of having to consciously hold position such as gripping the seat of a chair while being bent over it, bondage had taken away that responsibility and freed her up to simply be in the moment. The unexpected bonus was that when she pulled against the restraints it upped the intensity and converted the pain into...something, she still quite didn't know what. What she did know was that when she was permitted orgasm afterwards it exceeded anything she had ever experienced via conventional sex. Would fighting like that against restraints while receiving harder spankings, caning even, produce even greater highs for her? Surely there must be limits to what she could actually tolerate, but she knew she could definitely take more. Rebecca suddenly felt tingly between her legs and her right hand, seemingly with a mind of its own, moved to investigate while her left latched onto the edge of the countertop. She closed her eyes. The fact she was still tender down there was to be of no impediment to her at all.

Don's email later in the day addressed the subject that continued to dominate Rebecca's thoughts. Was she that predictable? "No," Rebecca muttered to herself. "He really is a mind reader."

The text of the message told her that in their next session she would progress to a more complete bondage situation; she would be restrained from moving her ankles as well as her wrists. Don would then be taking her to what he called her 'edge' with the goal of the session being to determine precisely where that edge might be. She had no qualms; in this regard Don knew her perhaps better than she knew herself. Although there were other correspondences between them, she re-read that same email every day for the next three days. Then it was Wednesday.

"Come on in Rebecca." Don closed the door behind her, took her hand in his and proceeded to sit down on the staircase while she remained standing in front of him in the hallway. She could tell by where he was looking that he approved of her short skirt. Don's eyes slowly moved up her body until they made contact with hers. "Ready?" he asked.

She was more than ready.

Don leaned sideways onto one of the steps and calmly issued his single-word instruction; "Strip."

Rebecca immediately kicked off her shoes and slid the blue lightweight sweater up and over her head. She was not wearing a bra; that was always his preference and her pert 32 Bs really didn't need one anyway.

"Closet," Don said in response to her quick looking around for a place to put the garment, and then nodded for her to proceed when she once again stood in front of him. She first pulled the blue jean skirt up to her waist to model her black lace panties for him and it remained there while she unfastened it from the side. Once the skirt was hanging in the closet, she quickly slipped the panties off and stood attentively for him with her hands behind her back. Rebecca had become very comfortable displaying herself naked in front of Don and she always enjoyed his unapologetic ogling of her body. It was several minutes before he cracked a smile, nodded and rose to his feet. Right hand on her bottom, he ushered her down the hallway into the living room. The five restraints were laid out as before, accompanied by a thin switch lying next to them.

Don first put the collar around Rebecca's neck and then sat on the couch and attached the wristbands before leaning forward, picking up the switch and brandishing it in the air. A one sided smile accompanied the quick flick of his wrist which caused the switch to emit its delightful whooshing sound but, rather than land it across her bottom, Don gently tapped the switch twice against Rebecca's upper left thigh and ordered her to step up on top of the coffee table.

"Feet apart and hands on your head, that's a good girl."

Rebecca loved Don telling her she was a good girl and she tried her utmost to keep obediently still while he attached the ankle restraints, but anticipation was causing her to sway slightly back and forth. Thankfully, Don stood up as soon as the ankle bands were in place and, taking her hand, assisted her to step down.

"We're going upstairs now," he told her. "Where I'm going to tie you spread-eagled onto the bed."

Don's words instantly caused Rebecca's eyes to widen and, trembling excitedly, she grasped the banister for support while she slowly ascended the stairs. Don, switch in hand, followed closely behind her and light taps from the switch directed her to the correct room.

The bed was covered with a white sheet and there was a shiny metal clasp attached to a black strap at each corner. Rebecca excitedly lunged forward, placed her hands flat on the bed and started to raise her right knee but Don's hands were suddenly on her shoulders. "We can't have you getting on the bed without a warm-up," he said softly. His right hand eased her leg back to the floor, so she was standing up against the waist-high mattress. His hands then brought hers together in front of her and clipped the wristbands together. "First, I'm going to have you bend over," he whispered into her right ear, then eased her forward so she was flat on the sheet from the waist up with her wrists bound together above her head. Don placed his left hand on the back of her neck, assuring she maintained that position while he administered a dozen warm-ups to her buttocks with the flat of his right.

"Now you can go on up," he told her, his hands squeezing her warm bottom cheeks while simultaneously pushing to help her. His fingers brushed against her vagina as Rebecca lifted her leg to clamber onto the mattress and she thought to linger in that leg-up position hoping for more touching, but Don picked up the switch and lightly stroked her back with it, encouraging her to crawl up onto the bed using her knees and elbows. "That's right," he said, "lie face down."

Rebecca murmured as she felt her legs being spread apart and the clasps attached; her clitoris was happily being pressed against the sheet. Don then unfastened her wrists and attached them to the other two corners of the bed before walking around and tightening each of the four straps to pull her into a well secured, spread-eagled position.

The whoosh of the switch was followed by a stinging sensation across her buttocks, but Rebecca's involuntary flinch was suppressed by the restraints. She closed her eyes; no longer need she be conscious of her reactions and try to control them, she could instead let them run rampant safe in the knowledge that the bonds would hold. The bonds had freed her so she could fully experience the sensations; to feel.

Don administered a full dozen strokes of the switch before setting it aside and massaging her flaming bottom, fingers on the cheeks and a thumb each side of her pussy so that each squeeze spread her apart; stimulation to further fuel her already hot desire but strategically insufficient to satisfy.

Don slid his fingertips down the inside of Rebecca's thighs and moved to stand at the left side of the bed. "Spanking time," he announced. "This is where we find your edge."

Rebecca began to pant; it was amazing how mere words could so inflame her arousal. Perhaps it was Don's accent?

The first slap was hard causing Rebecca to simultaneously pull her arms against the restraints and raise her head up off the bed as far as she was able. "It's okay," Don said with a soothing voice, adding "You can writhe against it all you like and I'll even help you with the head movement," as he placed his left hand cross the back of her neck. The next spank was equally as hard but the hand on her neck kept Rebecca nicely immobilized and, after maybe the seventh or eighth stroke...the count was becoming blurry for her...Rebecca's body became more complacent. Continuing spanking, Don slid his hand off her neck, stroked the side of her face and positioned it beneath her quivering chin. When his index finger brushed her lower lip she opened her mouth and allowed the finger to lie across her lower teeth, covering it with her hot breath with every grunting pant. She could hear the spanking and theorized that it must hurt because of the vibrations of her jaw, but she registered no knowledge of pain. She perceived heat; she perceived the need to be brought to orgasm, but there was nothing else. Suddenly the spanking stopped, Don's hand was gone from her chin and there were multiple fingers inside her, but she was unable to move herself against them. Don had complete control. Her moaning increased in both pitch and volume as his fingers proceeded to stimulate multiple points within her vagina as if she were a musical instrument. He played her into an unbelievable state of uncontrollable gasps and shudders. If she were not bound, she most surely would have been curled into a shuddering ball with her thighs squeezing the life out of Don's hand. Suddenly, a guttural scream accompanied by a surge of soaking warmth announced her satisfaction to the world. Did that sound come from her?

Don first caressed her flaming buttocks, soothing the fire with her moisture, and then unfastened the straps at the four corners of the bed but Rebecca just continued to lay face down and limpid as she attempted to recapture her breathing. He rolled her over and lay down next to her, enveloped her shoulders in his left arm, and cuddled her silently until she was able to raise her head up and smile at him. "Okay?" Don asked, brushing the hair from Rebecca's face and tucking it behind her left ear.

"That was incredible." Her voice came out as little more than a whisper, so she took a cleansing breath to further restore it. "I never would have thought I could take such as spanking as that. In fact, I don't think I could have taken even a stroke more before bursting into tears."

"That's your edge." Don nuzzled into Rebecca's raven hair as he spoke.

"And how do you know?" She wasn't really able to formulate the question, but Don understood. "I can tell," he answered and smiled at her. "I'm constantly monitoring you." He slid his hand over her thigh and stroked the series of small raised lines left by the switch on her crimson bottom. "You're going to be a bit sore and these marks are going to be around for the next day or so, you know. Is that going to be a problem at home?"

"No problem at all. I always wear a nightgown so no-one can see and if Nick wants sex, he just pulls it up and climbs on top after we're already in bed."

"Only ever in bed?"

"And only ever in missionary position, and he never touches my bottom." Rebecca grinned. "Besides, sex is so much better before the marks go away."

"True," Don nodded in agreement, then broke into a smirk and eased her onto her back. "And the more you receive the longer the effects will last." He touched his index finger to her still engorged clitoris. "But what about when your vagina is sore too?"

"It's never that sore," she instantly blurted out then, slightly embarrassed, buried her face into Don.

"Really," Don teased her both verbally and with light vibrations of his finger. "Because after being taken to your edge like that you're going to be in a constant stare of arousal for at least the rest of the day, so if I don't give you a few more orgasms now you'll be furiously masturbating at home. Either way, you're going to have a sore pussy at bedtime tonight."

"I'd rather it be you."

"Naughty girl," Don said jovially while stretching her arm out and clasping it to the corner of the bed, adding, "As you wish," as a faux warning.

Within minutes Rebecca was spread-eagled on her back, her smooth wanting pussy on full display and twitching in anticipation.

"Let's begin clitorally," Don said as she sat on the side of the bed, watching Rebecca's mouth open wider and wider and he roughed her clitoris up with two fingers. "Someone likes it hard," he teased as she moaned out an orgasm and then quickly slid a finger inside her before she could properly recover. "G-spot time," he added, his fingertip dancing on the telltale raised area just inside of her. Rebecca grunted rhythmically until he finally pressed the spot. "There you go."

Don gave Rebecca a few minutes to catch her breath before telling her she was next going to make her cum with a double, both clitoris and g-spot simultaneously. Her next orgasm happened even before he had fully inserted his middle and index fingers, so he produced another immediately afterwards by closing his hand which forced his thumb to press down onto her engorged clit.

As Don had promised, Rebecca was quite sore both front and back that night. But it didn't matter. Yes, it hurt when Nick entered her, but after only a few seconds she was rescued by the residual heat from Don's spanking and was able to participate in and even enjoy conventional sex with her husband; tame as it was.

13. Chapter Thirteen: Forced

REBECCA OFTEN PONDERED the whys of erotica, whether it was in the things she read, the disciplining she discreetly watched on the internet or increasingly intense activities she participated in with Don. She knew what the things that aroused her were but never could come to terms with the reason, especially things that many people would find abhorrent. She was quite certain, for instance, that the majority of happily married suburban housewives didn't secretly meet with men to be tied up, spanked and forced to orgasm. Still, not only had she learned to accept her idiosyncrasies, but she recognized they were actually needs without which she would be frustrated and, thereby, unable to be such a happily housewife. Rebecca smirked; didn't she owe that much to Nick? It was as much her responsibility to do what it took so she could be a good wife for him as it was for him to go to work in order to be a good provider.

Today's thought, why is it that being partially dressed is more erotic than being completely naked, was initially stimulated by Rebecca watching women being spanked on the internet and further developed by what she realized were her own turn-ons. Hand fidgeting between her thighs, she resolved to go to a fetish store and purchase something that Don might let her wear be spanked in: black fishnet stockings. He would be sure to like them and Rebecca wanted to do something for him too. Don had been more than a gentleman in the past two sessions in allowing them to be completely about her until her comfort with being restrained had been established. Now that she had been sufficiently indoctrinated into the world of bondage, he had told her he was going to resume using her orally with the next session, but she still felt the need to do something extra. Actually, when she was perfectly honest with herself, she was going to dress like this because she wanted Don to become sexually aroused by her.

When it came to making the purchase, Rebecca was delighted to also find matching arm-warmers which were like elbow length gloves but instead of covering her hands there was a loop that went around her middle finger to keep them from riding up her arms. She also couldn't resist completing the ensemble with a pair of thick-soled black leather heels which laced around silver studs in the front. They reminded her of Don's restraints. After all, what woman can pass up a pair of shoes that jump out at her like that?

The rain had been falling hard all day and when Don opened the front door he was greeted by a bedraggled looking Rebecca who thought she could quickly dash from her car without an umbrella and, instead, ended up standing on his stoop with thoroughly drenched hair. "Let me get you a towel," he said jovially, ushering her into the foyer and leaving her dripping on the mat. He was back quickly and gave her hair a quick rub with the towel, then slung it over his shoulder and began to unbutton her raincoat while she stood still with her arms by her side. Don smiled when he uncovered her erect nipples, a smile which broadened in approval when unfastening the second to last button exposed the smooth slit between her legs, but when he slid her coat off her and saw the 'outfit' the expression that followed was perfect. Rebecca beamed; she was thrilled with Don's visually rewarding response. Coat on the hanger, Don silently took the towel off his shoulder and set about a more thorough rubbing of her hair, ostensibly to dry it. His real motivation became quite apparent, however, when he quickly draped it around Rebecca's neck like a scarf and used it to pull her down to her knees. She offered no resistance.

Stroking the right side of her face against the firmness in the front of Don's pants, Rebecca delighted in the realization that her new outfit had accomplished the goal she'd set for it.

Left hand firmly holding the towel like a tie, Don wrestled with his right to unfasten his belt, buttons and hastily unzip his pants, releasing them to fall around his ankles, whereupon Rebecca raised her eyes and made a long, upward lick across the front of his black underwear. Did she really feel him pulsing beneath the soft cotton or was that her own excitement?

Don slid the front of his underwear down to reveal his erection and Rebecca repeated the lick up the full length of his exposed shaft, still looking upward to take in the pleasure in his eyes; pleasure that she was providing for him. His right hand moved to pull back his foreskin and direct the bulbous purple head to moisten her lips with his ample pre-cum. Eyes remaining in place, Rebecca slid her lips over him until they made contact with the retracted foreskin and proceeded to treat his frenulum to wild gyrations of the tip of her eager tongue. This was the first time she had ever seen Don gasp involuntarily and in response to his sudden uncontrolled thrusting back and forth she sucked his penis halfway into her mouth as if it were an extra thick milkshake. Don's cock pulsed between her tongue and the roof of her mouth as the fingers of his free hand buried themselves wildly in her still wet hair. His moan was a symphony to her ears and she greedily swallowed and sucked until his hands indicated his satisfaction by easing their grip, permitting her the freedom to bob her head back and forth up and down his well pleasured rod until he withdrew it from her mouth.

Don took Rebecca's hands in his, eased her to her feet and pulled up his pants before either of them spoke. He began with, "I like your outfit."

"*No kidding*," was the flippant response that remained in Rebecca's head. What came out instead was a demure, "Thank you."

Don slid the towel away and hung it on the umbrella stand next to her coat, then put his arm around her shoulders. "Come on in," he said, and escorted her into the living room.

Don sat Rebecca on the edge of the coffee table in order to attach the now familiar leather collar around her neck and then stood her up before securing the restraints around her wrists. "I see you noticed the belt," he said to her; she was clearly staring at a new object on the table. "It's called a bondage belt." He held it up with both hands so she could see the metal rings and the long thin strap hanging from it. "I'll show you how it works."

Don buckled the belt around Rebecca's waist with a ring positioned above each of her hips and the strap hanging down from the back. There was another ring in the front at the buckle. "Put your hands on your bottom," he instructed.

Rebecca watched intently as he fed the strap between her legs and slipped it through the ring at the buckle and, as Don snugged it up, she instinctively knew she was to pull her bottom cheeks apart so the strap could ease between them. Don gave it a slight tug, forcing a smile from Rebecca as the thin fabric slid between her labia lips and pressed against her clitoris. "Now then," he said, still holding the strap. "You notice this little slider at the end?"

Rebecca nodded rapidly. She was intrigued.

"This enables me to adjust the tightness, whether I clip it to your waist or," he fed the end through the ring on her collar, "Here. Head forward, there's a good girl."

Rebecca looked down and Don tightened the strap.

"Now then, see what happens if you pick your head up."

She slowly raised her head causing the strap to tighten between her legs, like a thong pulled up way too high, and immediately bent her head back down. "I do see," she said.

"Very good," Don nodded and attached the clip on each wristband to the corresponding rings on the belt. "And now, as you can see, your arms are nicely restrained by your sides." He picked up the crop and sat on the couch with Rebecca standing sideways to him. Thwack, the crop impacted her right buttock with a particularly sharp sting and Rebecca's involuntary jerk pulled the strap tightly between her pussy lips and it remained between them even after she put her head back down. She moved her hips in a slight side to side motion to make it wiggle against her clit while Don continued his cropping until her bottom was reddened to his satisfaction. It was when he made her walk across the room, however, that she really became stimulated, so much so that she was audibly panting and her knees were about to fail her.

"You'd better kneel down," Don said, standing behind her with his hands holding her arms and eased her to the floor in front of his armchair. Leaning forward in this position reduced the tension on the strap, but it was still enveloped by her labia lips. She had guessed that more oral was to ensue so was not surprised when Don sat down without his pants on and spread his legs. He took her head in both hands. "You did a wonderful job earlier," he told her, "But then you were giving pleasure. As we move further into bondage scenarios, however, I will be taking my pleasure rather than have you giving it."

Rebecca understood what he meant when he told her to simply open her mouth and he pushed his cock inside, straight back. When she felt it touch the back of her tongue, she immediately closed her mouth around it, attempting to suck, but Don pulled it back out. "Just be passive with your mouth open until I tell you otherwise," he told her, then shoved his erection back across her tongue and pushed her head back and forth, each thrust a bit deeper. She gagged and Don instantly withdrew.

"I'm sorry," she said. "I couldn't help it. Please may I try again?"

Don slid his penis back into her compliantly open mouth, but only halfway, and with his left hand still holding her head he slowly stroked himself as he spoke. "It's okay," he said in a comforting tone, "This is a new activity for you so there's going to be a natural learning curve."

His breathing was becoming more rapid, but he managed to maintain control of his speech while his right hand moved faster. "So for now I'm going to let you close your mouth."

Having him masturbate into her mouth was incredibly arousing for Rebecca, and even though Don's ejaculation was not as voluminous as earlier she was nevertheless more than eager to gulp it down. Watching him and swallowing his cum with every movement pulling against the strap stimulating her clitoris had left her incredibly squirmy, something which hadn't escaped Don's notice. He reached over and disconnected the strap from her collar then unsnapped her right wrist from the belt, holding it in his firm grip while he unsnapped her left, and then connected her wrists together and attached them to the ring on her collar.

Don stood up, moved behind her and Rebecca felt the strap slowly peel away, first from her pussy and then from the crack in her behind. Hands on her shoulders pushed her forward and her upper body was lying on her arms, flat on the seat of the armchair. Don's hand on the back of her neck made sure she would remain there. Rebecca gasped, there were fingers toying with her clit, and then there were fingers wriggling inside her. Don held her down as she pushed against him, then pulled his soaked hand from between her legs and slapped it hard onto her left bottom cheek. Successive strokes had Rebecca grunting, her pitch higher with each slap until her voice was reduced to a squeaky whimpering and her resistance against Don subsided. "That's better," he told her as his fingers once again invaded her compliant pussy. Her orgasm was instant.

Recovered, Rebecca sat with Don in his kitchen enjoying tea and biscuits. "I'm really sorry about earlier," she said. "I want so much to be able to do what you want but I have this horrible gag reflex." A coy smile suddenly captured her face as she continued with, "And I don't have any experience at this."

"If you are willing to learn, it's quite easy for you to overcome your reflexes. It's more a matter of wanting to and relaxing."

"Oh, I really do want to. Do you think I can?"

"I have every confidence in you, Rebecca." Don smiled and poured their second cups of tea.

14. Chapter Fourteen: Needs

HAND DIGGING EXCITEDLY around the bottom of her underwear drawer, Rebecca retrieved her vibrator. She had no idea whether her having it was really a secret or not. If her husband did know about it he had never said anything, which was probably best because she was sure Nick would only provide her with condemnation and disapproval. Early in their marriage she had fantasized about using it in front of him while he watched her, but peripheral queries around the subject quickly made her realize that was not to be. In the past few months since she had met Don she had actually had little use for it, but today it was to be put to a new purpose. She lay back on the bed with a pillow under her neck for support, closed her eyes and placed the tip of the vibrator against her parted lips. She would have to lubricate it with her tongue to enhance the simulation, but that was certainly not going to be problem. When it was sufficiently wet, she opened her mouth as wide as was comfortable, stuck her tongue out and slid the vibrator back along it while exhaling. Her research into the subject of how to perform deep throat had been extensive and breathing correctly was an integral part of the process. The end of the vibrator crossed the back of her tongue and entered her throat without her gagging. Rebecca was so proud; these daily exercises would have her ready for Don to use in no time. She slid the vibrator forward into her mouth and then back a bit deeper into her throat, determined to teach herself to remain relaxed when her airflow was cut off. She would trust Don to permit her the opportunities necessary for her to breathe; her role was simply to make herself available for him to take his pleasure. When she first performed orally on him it may have been as a quid-pro-quo for the spanking but that feeling and long since gone and now she genuinely wanted him to take her this way although she had no inkling as to why his doing this to her excited her so much. Rebecca grinned as she began to think about what was in store for her. The vibrator suddenly became endowed with a will of its own and before she realized it had slid from her mouth and maneuvered itself between her widely parted legs.

Naked except for her fishnets on her arms and legs, Rebecca stood silently in Don's living room that following Wednesday while he attached restraints to her neck, wrists and ankles. The promise of today's session was more involved bondage and even harder spankings followed by repeated orgasms before he was to use her. She could hardly wait.

Don led her upstairs and ordered her to bend over the bed with her hands above her head. She watched excitedly, chin against the sheet, while he attached her wrists to the upper two corners of the bed before he picked up a cane from the top of the dresser. She loved the sound a cane makes prior to impact and it had been so long since she had experienced it, the last time was when she role playing a schoolgirl.

"Six strokes should provide a decent warming up," he said talking to the cane in his right hand while Rebecca's brain was silently screaming out, "Yes, yes, yes."

After a cursory swish in the air, Don turned to address Rebecca. "Be a good girl and count them out for me."

Dreamily compliant and willing to do just about anything to hear Don call her a good girl, Rebecca closed her eyes in anticipation of the whoosh and then dug her fingers into the sheet as she exhaled the word, "One," immediately following the initial stroke. He had, clearly, gone easier on her when he was in the role of the headmaster. The sting had yet to reach its peak before the second blow landed half an inch beneath the first and by the count of four her bottom was already throbbing. When she managed to eke out, "Six," through erratic breaths her whole bottom was on fire and the restraints around her wrists served to emphasize through denial how much she would have liked to rub it, denial which required conscious effort after Don had untied her and told her to climb onto the bed. Thankfully, she was not unrestrained for long. Don soon had Rebecca over on her back with arms and legs up in the air, her ankles and wrists clamped to a small device comprised of four metal rings held together with leather. He called it a hog tie. The results of Don's handiwork with the cane were now prominently on display as was Rebecca's obviously aroused labia, parted by engorgement to reveal her excited pink inner lips. A single, gentle upward motion of Don's hand across them provided him with ample moisture to subsequently soothe both sides of her buttocks. "Now you're ready for your spanking," he told her, his fingers gliding across the six parallel ridges as if they were a series of speed bumps.

Left hand around Rebecca's right calf to prevent her from rolling, Don stood next to the bed and delivered a single loud slap to her left bottom cheek. The glow was instant. An equally strong blow to the other side followed close behind and Don then paused to visually examine the redness. Satisfied, he began a lighter series of slaps alternating from side to side as if Rebecca's bottom were bongo drums. When her open-mouthed breathing became accompanied by short grunts Don changed the tone to staccato until her pitch was barely audible and her eyelids were aquiver. "I believe we're almost there," he announced without emotion, then stopped spanking and shoved four fingers directly into her until the base of his thumb pushed onto her clitoris. Her scream of delight was deafening, and it took a full minute before Don needed to move his fingers to keep her going. He completed the orgasmic series by sliding his hand back until the tips of his index and forefingers were on top of her g-spot and with the tip of his thumb on her clit he simply squeezed.

"More?" Don teased.

"No," Rebecca sputtered as soon as she recovered her voice. "Please, no more."

"What then?"

"Fuck my mouth." Did those words really come from her? They were so unladylike. Rebecca didn't care.

Don rocked her forward and positioned a pillow underneath her shoulders. She allowed her head flop back while he straddled her face and looked up at the erection being positioned above her. Don was, clearly, as excited as she was about this.

"Open your mouth," he instructed as his right hand retracted his foreskin. "Wide."

Rebecca exhaled and simultaneously pushed her tongue out as the slippery head of Don's cock slid along it. He paused for a few seconds as it entered her throat and then slid it back an inch. Hands on each side of Rebecca's head ensured that there would be no side to side movement on her part. He pushed back in, a little deeper this time, and for a little longer. This was going perfectly, but Don's balls brushing against her face and his moans of pleasure being the equivalent of telling Rebecca she was being a good girl caused her to lose concentration and the next time Don pulled back she closed her mouth around his cock, instinctively wanting to suck him. Suddenly her tongue was in the back of her mouth, panicking and trying to push him out, and a retching sound was accompanied by the horrible feeling of being about to throw up. Don instantly pulled out of her mouth and rolled her onto her left side while he quickly unclipped the restraints.

"I'm so sorry." Rebecca was panting; the realization that she had obviously disappointed Don almost had her in tears.

Don sat on the bed next to her and caressed her hair with his fingertips. "You made a truly valiant effort," he told her soothingly.

"Do you want to try again?" She looked up at him with saucer eyes. "Please? I want you to. Force me to take it, even if I do gag. I want you to be pleased with me."

"Not today. Once a gag reflex kicks in you'll be shot for the rest of the day. Besides, I don't want you gagging; I want you to be comfortable." Don pulled her in for a reassuring hug. "It's okay."

"Really?" Rebecca's sheepishness underscored how much she needed to hear that.

"Really; now let's get dressed and have a cup of tea."

"I feel like such a failure," Rebecca admitted while she cradled the teacup. "I completely lost myself in the moment and my mouth just closed. Is there any way you can make me keep it open?"

"Don't worry, Rebecca. In the wonderful world of BDSM there are a wide variety of tools available, and devices for helping you keep your mouth open are really quite common. I'll pick one up before our next session and we can try again."

BDSM; the phrase bounced around inside Rebecca's head for the rest of the day. It was the explanation she had been searching for. She had always known her dark desires were more than for just sexual gratification, but she had never made the connection before. She was a masochist, and Don has been providing her with just the right amount of sadism all along. Who else but a sadist would tie a woman up and shove his cock down her throat, and what woman who wasn't a masochist would want it done to her. Not just with any man, though. Don was truly special. Rebecca grinned; in spite of what had happened today she really, really still wanted him to deep throat her after her next spanking. She wanted it almost as much as she wanted that next spanking. Hell, it might even be a need.

15. Chapter Fifteen: Subspace

TWO DAYS LATER REBECCA still had welts across her bottom. They made her happy, bringing back the delicious memory of how they had come about. She thought back on how she had then been trussed up and spanked to the brink of tears before being given the release of orgasm, repeatedly, over which she had no control. Her heart rate accelerated with the recollection.

Her throat had been a little sore yesterday, as Don told her it might be, but was fine now so she decided to practice relaxing while taking her vibrator in to where it blocked her airway. She would do this every day. Plus, if Don came up with a tool to force her to keep her mouth open then things would go just fine next time. What began as a simple spanking had evolved into BDSM and the more she was immersed into these activities, the more she relinquished control to Don, the greater the intensity of her experience. Most women would be frightened by the path she was on, but all Rebecca could think about was the earnestness of her craving, her need. She had also come up with a couple of questions, perhaps they were more observations, about how things were developing; questions that were more effectively discussed in person rather than by email. In spite of this being a busy week for Don, he was happy to meet with her that Friday to discuss them. But their meeting had to be limited to the lunch hour, so they decided on a restaurant close to where he was working that day.

Rebecca arrived at the restaurant early and she sat in the waiting area watching for him. Even though they were just meeting for chat she still dressed with Don in mind, wearing a short skirt and a sheer blouse. She would have gone without a bra but knew that doing so would make her too self-conscious in a public setting, so she elected to wear a pretty flowered one that matched her panties. Don wouldn't be seeing them, of course, but knowing she was following his rules was strangely warming.

Don came in wearing dark pinstripes with a gold and black silk tie; a power suit made her wonder just what sort of consulting he did. He smiled at her, and as soon as she had risen to her feet he addressed the hostess. For the first time since she had met him Rebecca realized that Don was a man who exercised control over every aspect of his life.

The first thing Rebecca wanted to discuss was what Don called her edge, the point at which she had taken as much spanking as she was able. It was by no means a static point, each time taking longer to reach, and was probably best described as the point right before she was about to burst into tears; something that Don appeared to instinctively be in tune with. She was also instantly orgasmic when touched at that point, and there was the crux of her question. "What would happen," she asked, "If you kept on going?"

"Spank you over the edge, you mean?" Don's eyes sparkled blue.

"What aren't you telling me?" Rebecca could tell by Don's expression that he knew precisely what she wanted to know but he was going to make her ask all the same. "Is there release to be had in tears?"

"For a true spankee, yes there is. If properly taken over her edge a spankee will achieve orgasm from continued spanking without needing to be touched," he grinned and indicated with his eyes, "Down there." Don quickly raised his right hand to cut off her words. "Yes, you do have the attributes of a true spankee," he said, answering the question it was not necessary for Rebecca to ask.

Rebecca could hardly contain herself and leaned, almost lunged, across the table to ask in a loud whisper, "What do we have to do?" Darn it that Don had to go back to work soon, she wanted to go to his house right then. Her thighs were tapping together excitedly.

"I'm afraid you're your own impediment to that happening at the moment," Don spoke calmly and waited for Rebecca to quizzically settle back in her seat before continuing. "Do you remember the first time you were tied and spanked, how you seemed to zone out and lose time?"

"Yes, of course. It was wonderful." Rebecca was aghast, this was the other thing she wanted to discuss with Don and yet here he was bringing it up seemingly out of context. How could these things be related? He had just said that she was her own impediment. Had she done something wrong?

"Even though you've been more tightly bound, and the intensity of your spankings has subsequently increased, you haven't experienced that again, have you?"

"No." Rebecca took a long drink of iced tea, almost afraid to but nevertheless needing to ask, "Why is that?"

"Because the first time you were disconnected and completely in the moment; with thought turned off like that you were able to just respond to what I was doing with you and you slipped into what is called subspace. It is in subspace that a spankee can be successfully taken over her edge. The last couple of times you were preoccupied, most likely with trepidation of my taking you orally I suspect. The fact is, if you don't release yourself from thinking I won't be able to place you into subspace and you won't be able to experience the highlights of a true spankee."

"You're a hundred percent right about where my mind has been the past couple of times," Rebecca admitted. Of course he was. "But if we got that out of the way first, wouldn't we be able to..." her voice faded away as Don slowly shook his head.

"That's not the way it works," he told her. "I need to simply remove that worry from you. Come to our next session with no expectations of anything happening, no demands upon you. Free your mind so you can be in the moment."

"But I want you to be pleased with me." Rebecca objected, quickly looking around to ensure that none of the other diners were listening to her before continuing with, "I want you to be able to deep throat me."

"How about if we get you to spankee status first," Don hooked her chin with his index finger and forced her to look up at him. "You'll simply have to relax trust me, okay?"

"Okay." Rebecca had no control over her excited grin. "I can do that."

Rebecca dressed in the same clothes she had worn at their lunch a few days prior, with the exception being she did not have a bra on so she could tempt Don with teasing glimpses of her nipples. On arriving at his house Don took her into the living room where, instead of restraints, there was a bottle of mead and two earthenware beakers on the coffee table. "Sit down and relax," Don instructed as he reached for the bottle. "You'll like this."

They sat back on the couch to enjoy the drink and Rebecca sat sideways so Don could see up her skirt, something he was not shy about doing. When they had finished quaffing the honey wine Don placed the mugs back on the table and told her to stand up then, after looking at her for two or three minutes, rose from the couch himself. He positioned himself behind her and whispered for her to keep still, that he was going to undress her. She liked his hands on her, removing her clothes, and once she was naked Rebecca ascended the stairs with Don closely behind, directing her. All the restraints were set out on the dresser top, but Don only affixed the wrist bands and the bondage belt to her before ordering her to lie face down on the bed, her hands above her head. He tied her wrists to a single rope which looped around the center of the headboard and pulled it taut, then lay down next to her and gently stroked the long hair that cascaded across her shoulders. "Close your eyes," he whispered in an incredibly soothing voice. No problem at all. The combination of mead, Don's touch, and the security of the restraints had already transported her to a semi-dreamlike state.

"I'm going to spank you now," Don continued using the same hypnotic voice while his right hand slowly made its way down her back and began to caress her buttocks. The caresses became squeezes and then evolved into light spankings. The only sound other than Don's hand connecting with naked flesh was from Rebecca's soft purring; her body remaining complacent, seemingly unaware of the increasing intensity until it was belied by the innocent separating of her legs and twitch tightening of her rosy buttocks. The spanking became louder, but Rebecca felt only warmth and a strange contentment. Were those hard, breathy sounds coming from her? The spanking was continuing harder and harder and Don was lying next to her, his left hand softly caressing her cheek, her parted lips, while his right continued with the pounding. She felt his breath in her hair. She was completely on fire from the waist down. There were only short breaths now, but her body had become strangely limpid and was not fighting against the bonds. A high-pitched sound suddenly surrounded her head and she couldn't close her mouth, then her entire body shuddered into a cascade of tears and ecstasy. Was she crying or coming? Paralyzed by wave upon wave of orgasm, all she could do is feel. And feel she did. A way she had never felt before. A feeling that remained after Don stopped spanking, untied her pliable body and rolled her over. Barely aware of his movements around her, she delighted in this state of disconnect, her mind completely blank and having no desire to engage it. After all, Don had control of the situation, whatever it might be. Her arms were now restrained by her sides. That was fine. Her wrists were bound together but strategically placed such that her fingers had contact with her pussy, if she wished. But at this moment she wished for nothing. Her happy smile as Don caressed her face offered no resistance to whatever it was that was being placed between her lips. The tightening of the bands around the back of her head ensured her mouth was to stay wide open and, while aware, she paid no mind to the flow of drool trickling down her neck. It was only when Don pushed his cock through the ring and into her throat that her fingertips became activated and took her to simultaneous orgasm with him as hot cum flooded her mouth. Don then pulled out, removed the ring gag, and reassuringly held Rebecca. There was no rush, no time pressure and she slowly returned from subspace with a grateful smile, delighting in being permitted to orally pleasure Don as a means of thanking him. Rebecca had become a true spankee.